LETTER BOXES ARE RED

EDWARD THOMAS

Grosvenor House
Publishing Limited

This book is published by
Grosvenor House Publishing Ltd
Link House
140 The Broadway, Tolworth, Surrey, KT6 7HT.
www.grosvenorhousepublishing.co.uk

This book is a work of fiction. Any resemblance to
people or events, past or present, is purely coincidental.

A CIP record for this book
is available from the British Library

ISBN 978-1-83975-693-1

by the same author

Fiction

Slices of a Time

No Treat on Offer

Waltzes of Africa

Non-fiction

The Playhouse on the Park
   1st and 2nd editions

The Reluctant Star - Malcolm Vaughan

At the hour of midnight the Salerian gate was silently opened, and the inhabitants were awakened by the tremendous sound of the Gothic trumpet.

Edward Gibbon

The Decline and Fall of the Roman Empire

Chapter 1

Friday 24 June 2016

Henry Wagstaff woke up in a state of exhilaration not experienced for a long time in his seventy-six years. Before doing anything else, and entirely out of character, he went straight to his journal. Ignoring the lines on the page, again out of character, he wrote in large lettering: 'It has happened. It has truly happened. The UK has voted to leave the European Union.'

Impulse forced him to expand. He had stayed up all night hardly feeling sleepy, such was the disbelief he found himself experiencing. One after another the results showed, and with massive percentage majorities in some cases, that the Leave side had won. He was in front of the set at twenty minutes to five when David Dimbleby announced the BBC was forecasting that the UK had voted to leave the E.U.

Henry almost had to take hold of himself to view it with calmness. It was not until after six o'clock that he had gone to bed, daylight well to the fore, feeling what he described in his diary as 'sheer undiluted bloody euphoria'. We really were on the way to extricating ourselves from that controlling, self-indulgent, profligate outfit. The images of Keith Vaz looking as white as a sheet or of Paddy Ashdown proclaiming in a tweet: 'Our poor country!' could only add to the sense of unbelievable elation.

Events had moved fast. Henry had been in bed for only three hours yet during that time David Cameron had broadcast his resignation as Prime Minister. Henry classed that as excellent news in itself. He'd had more than sufficient of the man.

A few hours later he was back in his diary, having only just remembered to make a bread pudding for Mollie's birthday which he would take downstairs for the weekly Scrabble session with the sisters. He'd had an early lunch so that he would have time to record as much as he could of the day's momentous and entirely unexpected events.

'Since getting up,' he wrote, 'and it's still only one o'clock, a motion of No Confidence in the Government has been issued by Jeremy Corbyn. Nicola Sturgeon has said unequivocally that a second Scottish independence referendum will take place, Scotland having voted Remain.'

Henry was now in his stride. 'When one thinks of all that has been thrown at Vote Leave: all the bile, the patronising condescension, all the experts from economics, science, arts, everything and everybody, it is bloody marvellous. The establishment has received a good and well-deserved kicking.'

o o o

Henry's mood had not shifted an iota as he stepped out of his flat at three o'clock, a touch overloaded. He was carrying as usual Scrabble board and bag of tiles, baking tin with cooled-down bread pudding, his dictionary, and the day's *Telegraph* under his arm. He would play down his enthusiasm in case of dissension downstairs. He knew that Julia had voted Remain and Mollie Leave. So far neither had expressed especial enthusiasm for their respective sides. That was partly evidenced now as he realised, through their open door, that they were not discussing Europe. They were talking about him. By one floor up their conversation was muffled but Henry's hearing was acute.

'I do wonder why a chap like him has never married.'

Henry chuckled at Julia's observation and stopped in his tracks.

'I have a feeling he's asexual,' replied Mollie.

'A sexual what?' sniffed Julia, a trifle concerned at the way conversation was moving.

'No, Julia. Asexual. It's one word. It means someone not interested in either way, or any way.'

'Oh, I see.' Another sniff from Julia.

Mollie was not finished. 'I've often wondered about his high-pitched voice, always ready to crack. Like Anne Widdecombe's. He might well have had an accident when he was very young, or his balls hadn't dropped properly.'

'*Mollie!*' This was getting too much for Julia. For Mollie with her nursing background that she had embraced in the latter stages of her working life, such an observation seemed matter- of-fact.

The effect on Henry earwigging a floor above was one of near hilarity. Mollie had got it right on two counts. Matters that had caused him some embarrassment in younger days had no consequence in

3

older age. He had often wondered about his cracked voice but no doctor or hospital had ever discovered anything wrong.

He had never spoken to them about the other matter and would never think of doing so. He was indeed asexual, although the word had not seemed to enter the general lexicon until he was in his thirties. It was true that he was not interested in that way – as people expressed it – with either women or men. Nor had it worried him, on the basis that one never missed what one had never experienced. In fact when he saw relationships all around him collapsing like card packs, he felt he wasn't missing much. Henry's full life of work and interests had always kept him content. He was about to close his door when something the sisters were now saying caught his further attention.

'The one thing I do wish about Henry is that he would reduce his weight.'

'Oh, I agree,' replied Julia. 'It can't be healthy for him to carry all that weight around.'

Henry allowed himself a snort. This did touch a nerve. He had tried a number of times to reduce his weight, which had only increased in the years since he had stopped playing football. With irritation he had to admit to himself that he did like his food. He looked down at the bread pudding and resolved not to have a piece of it when offered by the sisters over a cup of tea.

But he refused to feel out of sorts on this day of otherwise undiluted elation. First though he contrived to let the sisters know he was on his way so that they would not be embarrassed at being caught talking about him. He therefore made a point of banging his door

4

shut and starting to whistle a happy tune loudly as he descended the stairs.

o o o

'You've done well there, Henry. How many is that on a triple score?'

Mollie Chadwick always congratulated Henry when he produced a seven-letter word. This time it was BLASTED, with a blank tile representing the D. Henry totalled up eighty-eight points but mumbled the answer to Mollie's question. He felt her sister resented large scores as Julia did not usually come up with them.

'Yes, that's good,' echoed Julia, trying hard. 'Three points more than Mollie's age today'.

Mollie laughed. Julia was capable of saying the wrong thing but she was certain this was not an unkind remark. Henry remained unsure. Julia was ready for an escape.

'The tea must be brewed now.' Julia extricated herself from the table they were sitting at next to the bay window and left the room. It was Mollie's turn and she bent over her tile rack.

'Do you think Julia gets much out of these sessions now?' Henry was becoming a bit concerned that Scrabble was not after all one of her pleasures.

'Oh certainly,' answered Mollie. 'She always says how she looks forward to it. Don't worry about Julia. She likes the stimulation of exerting her brain.'

Henry did not know so much but let it go.

'Well, Henry.' Mollie lowered her voice although she could hear plenty of Julia's clatter with the tea things in the kitchen. 'What about the Leave vote?'

'Still can't believe it,' replied Henry.

'I've tried to lay off the subject. Julia was content to say that she voted Remain for the sake of the status quo. Don't rock the boat – that sort of thing. But now she has started to bang on about the peace we've enjoyed all these years because of the European Union.'

Henry sniffed. 'Well, that's been down to Nato since the War. Does Julia forget we had peace for nearly thirty years before the Common Market came along, let alone the E.U. itself in 1992?'

'That's what gets to me,' echoed Mollie. 'I wouldn't have minded if we'd stayed as the Common Market. And I'm all for co-operation between any set of countries, I really am. I just don't want to be *controlled* by them.'

'Quite,' said Henry.

'Shh. Julia's coming in.'

'Any plans for your birthday evening?' Henry took the cue to change the subject.

'Julia's taking me to the theatre.'

'It's a good play. I'll be reviewing it while you're both watching it tonight.'

Julia was back in the room pushing a trolley.

'You're really absorbed with your hospital programme, Henry.' Mollie poured out the first cup and gave it to him. 'I know I've enjoyed the few times you've had me on it.'

'You must come again. You're good at talking about films.'

'Ah, well, not so much now. I don't care for the modern stuff. Much prefer the film society offerings.'

'Any time you're ready to join me again, say the word. The only problem these days is getting back here with the car at half past eleven. Parking in Chessington Gardens is becoming worse on a Friday night.'

It was then that Mollie spotted the bread pudding that was looking slightly different. 'How thoughtful of you, Julia, placing a candle in the middle of it.'

Julia took the pudding from the trolley and placed it on the table. 'I should have thought of buying proper birthday candles. I've had to make do with a thick red Christmas candle. Not really appropriate.'

'Never mind, dear.' Mollie overlooked the strange sight. 'It's the thought that counts. It makes a change from birthday cake, and we really do enjoy your bread pudding, Henry.'

Henry smiled. He knew that the sisters much preferred his culinary skills with bread pudding rather than cakes. 'Well, it gets away from Emma Thompson's stereotype about us.' The sisters groaned. 'What was it she called us? "A tiny little something corner of Europe, a cake-filled something grey old island". Makes you wonder why so many people want to come here if that's the case.'

'Now then, Henry. Let me cut a piece of your own delicious bread pudding.'

'Ah, no thank you, not this week.' Henry patted his stomach self-consciously.

Chapter 1a

Al-Jum'ah 18 Ramadan 1437

'I wonder if the Queen is still alive.'

Julia Chadwick's reflection competed with her concentration on what to try out next on the Scrabble board. Henry Wagstaff was looking down on his own rack at the time, contemplating where to place the useful S that had just turned up. He sighed inwardly at Julia's off-the-cuff remark. It was proving so true: Elisabeth Kubler-Ross's theory on grief. Five stages to go through. The last was acceptance. Henry was aware of a lot of acceptance both in Eastbourne and elsewhere that he would not have believed possible, even after fifteen years.

'She must be ninety now,' said Mollie.

'She was ninety in what used to be April,' offered Henry.

Mollie paid closer attention. 'Have you heard anything about her?'

'No, but she was born in 1926.'

'And the Duke is even older, if he's still with us.'

Still with us. Henry mused over and felt momentarily gladdened that quaint old expressions like that had not died out of the language, unlike so much else. 'Christian' was one word that had gone. We were all described as 'non-Muslims' now.

'I'm sure we would have heard. The Leader would have seen to it that something would go into the *English Arab News*.'

Henry sighed again. 'I expect they are still holed up in the Castle of Mey.' Henry knew that The Leader had a certain respect for the Queen and Philip. Their longevity qualified them for that. He still wondered though what had happened to most of the younger royals. Nothing was heard of them, except for the one or two who'd made it to America before the shutters came down. Henry continued to hope that the States might come to Europe's aid one day. Not that he was holding his breath. What was it Churchill was supposed to have said? 'The United States can always be relied upon to take the right action after exhausting all other possibilities.'

'There, that's the best I can do.' Julia placed HUGE down on the board. She counted up the number of points and Henry added it to his column of figures. He always kept the scores. The sisters had long decided he was the mathematician and they were glad not to have to bother. They noticed how meticulous he was, and would come downstairs to them each week with carefully ruled columns drawn on blank sheets of paper.

Henry became increasingly mindful of how he could place his own seven-letter word he had been nursing. Trying to control his excitement, for there was little of that these days, he placed on the board LORRIES, the E under Julia's H, the S under the U. He totted up his score and recorded it.

'I'll make some tea in a minute,' said Julia, 'and we'll drink to Mollie's birthday.'

Henry mused again, this time at the phrasal verb 'drink to'. Tea and other soft drinks were the only means one could deploy to 'drink to' now, except for the illicit stills in the cellars of those taking a considerable risk. He thought of the brandy he was still keeping for emergencies and wondered anew how secure it was.

'Are you quite sure it's today?' queried Mollie.

'I am'. Henry was just ruling off another set of lines while awaiting his next go. 'I still keep a regular tally on our calendar.'

'Do be careful, Henry. You could get fined for that.'

'Possibly. They'd have to delve deep in the cupboard. The diaries might have gone, but I'm determined the dates haven't.'

Julia laughed. 'Rest assured, Mollie. Knowing Henry's record-keeping, I checked with him. Today really is Friday 24 June in the year 2016, and you really are eighty-five.'

'Thank you, dear. I'm not sure I need to be reminded. Now then. I can't make a seven-letter word but I *can* get rid of this X that I've been holding on to for so long. There now.' Mollie laid down on the board the letters forming IBEXES.

'What ever's that?' said her startled sister.

'Ibexes are animals,' replied Mollie.

'Get away. I don't believe you.'

'Honestly, Julia. An ibex is a goat.'

'Well, I've never heard of it.'

Henry was already diving into his trusty old OED with the tattered covers. He was well accustomed now to settling disputes between the sisters by referring to the dictionary. Indeed it was the only way he could defend himself sometimes against Julia.

'Here it is,' he said, pointing. 'Ibex: a wild goat, and you can pluralise it the usual way.'

Julia tossed her head in the air. She did not take kindly to being proved wrong. 'I don't need to look. I believe you. I'll go and make some tea.' As she got up, her mood softened. 'And we'll have some of Henry's excellent bread pudding to mark Mollie's birthday.'

Henry winked at Mollie as Julia left the room.

'Another difficult moment over,' observed Mollie. 'In all of that, you've forgotten to mark me up for fifty-five points.'

'Oh, of course. Sorry.' Henry duly recorded the score.

'I was only thinking this morning when Julia wished me a happy birthday. I hadn't realised. Eighty-five today. Twenty years ago I was sixty-five. I could have done all sorts of things then that I can't now. Wish I could remember though what I did do that day.'

Henry Wagstaff dipped into pensive mood. 'If things had been the same, I could have said what I was doing through my journals.'

Mollie looked directly at him. She remembered how much store Henry had set by his journals. 'I wouldn't mind betting that's what you miss most.'

Henry thought for a moment. There was so much that he missed, but Mollie was right. 'It is,' he said shortly.'

'Why?'

'Oh, partly for the reason we've just been mentioning. I can no longer go back to check on what I was doing on specific days.' He sighed and paused for a moment. 'But they had to go, particularly for what I said in one of them in 1990, that got me ejected from the region where our current masters come from.'

Mollie knew the history, or thought she did. Henry had not told them the full story. She and Julia did not move to Chessington Gardens until a few years after Henry's unceremonious departure from Saudi Arabia but gradually they had come to hear something about it. 'When you look back, you must regard it as a misguided thing to have done.'

'Oh, it was daft. If I'd imagined for a moment that the *Eastbourne Herald* was going to print the whole lot verbatim, I wouldn't have sent it.' Henry laughed darkly. 'Even when I first saw the article, my first thought was not worry but annoyance with myself. All that raw diary entry stuff – the register was all wrong for a newspaper audience. To this day I'm amazed they printed the whole lot. So no, it was a fair cop. I should have thought more about the possible implications. In view of what's happened since, I'm only too thankful the Saudis themselves never knew about it. Good old Aeronautics UK with their £10 billion contract to supply arms and personnel. They saw to it they got rid of me before their cash cow got wind of it.'

It had been a long time since Henry had recalled vividly the mass shredding exercise he knew was needed when the Occupation occurred. Quite apart from the events referred to with Mollie, too much reflection had been included in the journals that would not have found favour if discovered. The fatwa announced against Salman Rushdie had occurred while he was working in Dhahran and Henry had expounded considerably on that alone. The journals were therefore the first to go from his life. It had taken him a full day to get rid of them. Thank God he had. It was only a week or so after that when the authorities began their extensive searches in people's property. His anger rose again at the impertinence and he had to shake himself out of it.

'What do you miss most, Mollie?'

'Cinemas first and theatres second. And without doubt, Glyndebourne. Oh God, how I still yearn for those evenings in long gowns out in the heart of the Sussex countryside. It would have been something like that I would have been doing twenty years ago. We hadn't been living here long but Julia treated me to an evening at the Devonshire Park and then kept up the habit until the Occupation. Or it was the Congress if the play wasn't up to much and there happened to be a concert on. That's right. It would have been one of those options. I'd forgotten for a moment. It all seems such a long time ago. Now look at those places, and the Hippodrome.' She sighed. 'It doesn't do to dwell on these things.'

Julia arrived, pushing the tea trolley. Henry got up to help her transfer the tea things to the table. He took special care with the bread pudding the sisters requested every week.

'Henry and I were just discussing, Julia, what were the things we miss from the old days. I can imagine what your answer would be.'

'Not so much now, but yes, I missed dreadfully being permitted to drive. I'd never been one much for women's lib, but really when they took away our right to get behind the wheel of a car, I'd have been ready for the barricades, until I saw what they were doing to the women who did protest.'

The threesome went quiet. It was Henry who lightened the mood.

'As a matter of fact, I spotted a small paragraph in the paper reporting that the Government in New Arabia is beginning discussions about possibly letting women drive cars over there.'

'There you are, Julia. You might even be able to get back to it.'

'Don't bank on it though,' warned Henry. 'Don't forget that it's the Wahhibis who are the boss there just as much as here; the most conservative force of Islam. While they're in charge, I can't see anything lenient getting through.'

Julia shrugged. 'In any case I'm too old now, and too out of touch.' She passed the two cups of tea she had just poured to her companions. As if from determination, Julia's mood changed.

'Let's look on the bright side. We've been stuck with it for years now. Think of the advantages.'

Henry blinked. 'Advantages?'

'Yes. Consider how much more secure we are now in Eastbourne. At night, for instance. You can walk through the town centre very late, even past groups of young lads, and you know for certain they won't cause the slightest trouble, especially with no alcohol anywhere in sight. And there are no young women with them to egg them on.'

'But Julia,' said an incredulous Mollie. 'You haven't been out at night for years.'

'No, well, that's what I've heard.'

Chapter 2

✿

Friday 11 November 2016

Along the western end of the sea front at Eastbourne, you come to Carlisle Road. Turning inland it winds its way past restaurants, shops and the Heritage Centre, before stopping itself on a diversion around the Congress Theatre. Then it takes back its name and marches up a gentle incline on tarmac long covering the South Downs. Towards its end is a memorial arch, saved as the last remnant of Ascham School. Fifty-one names of Old Boys lost in the First World War are inscribed on its stonework. Every eleventh of November a group of a dozen or so gathers in remembrance of them and of all souls perished in war.

On this Armistice Day two of the dozen gathered there were Henry Wagstaff and Mollie Chadwick. The latter had particular reason always to be there. In the lead-up to the two minutes' silence she was explaining herself to a woman she had not met before and who was intrigued as to why Mollie was attending.

'It's for the brother I lost. He was on the Burma railway and finally succumbed. Reggie was a good bit older than me. What about yourself?'

'Oh, I'm on holiday for a few days, staying at a guest house in Meads. The people there told me about the annual ceremony here so I came along. I'm fascinated that you all come to this small gathering rather than to a larger commemoration.'

'I dare say I shall go along to the main memorial on Sunday morning. But I never feel the sense of intimacy that I do here. I'm always closer to my brother when I come here.'

The woman smiled and the three of them introduced themselves to each other.

Joyce Grimshaw was from Battersea and said she frequently came to Eastbourne for short breaks, especially out of season. She claimed to enjoy the peace and quiet and roaming over the South Downs, although this particular day's weather was a bit too cold for it.

Henry was about to express agreement when they were cut short by the piper who announced that it was just coming up to eleven o'clock.

When the silence was over, the piper offered a prayer and then announced that the students from the campus across the road were making an invitation to everybody present to join them as their guests for coffee.

'What a charming idea!' exclaimed Joyce.

'They do this every year now,' said Henry. 'We always go over. Would you care to join us?'

'That would be delightful,' returned Joyce. 'And it'll be nice to get into the warm.'

'It is very cold this year. Usually we're lucky with the sun out,' said Mollie.

Led by the piper playing *Amazing Grace*, the threesome made their way the short distance across the road with some half dozen others through the tree-lined grounds to the Starting Gate, as the café bar was named.

'It's quite an astute move,' offered Mollie. 'There was a fair amount of dissension up here when the university was expanded a few years ago. Trouble with noise and extra cars parked, often late at night. The students have been building bridges, trying to bring residents and themselves together. This is one of the ways they've been doing it.'

The group entered the building and walked across an Edwardian hall into the café area where several young people were seated, their heads poised over laptops.

Joyce laughed. 'A bit different from our day. We'd have had endless sheets of paper and ballpoint pens.' A young man heard, looked up and smiled.

'Henry would know, but I wouldn't,' observed Mollie. 'I didn't go to university.'

'Forgive me if I've got it wrong,' said Joyce. 'Are you husband and wife?'

The other two laughed and Mollie explained that they were flat neighbours. Just as they were heading to the counter, having been invited by the young staff to accept coffee or whatever they wanted to drink, they heard a kerfuffle going on in one corner. A group of four was exhibiting a lot of anger, although all were in agreement.

'What I can't believe,' said a young woman with purple hair, 'is how stupid so many women must have been to vote for him.'

'Too right,' replied a male student, 'after hearing on microphone what he said he would do with that woman's pussy.'

The other young man in the group tapped him on the knee and shushed him, at the same time pointing to the clutch of elderly visitors suddenly in their midst. They lowered their voices.

Mollie allowed herself a laugh. 'Not as though we haven't heard it all before, but it's nice of them to be concerned about our feelings.'

'Yes, that's pretty good for these days,' echoed Henry. 'Nonetheless, that student has got it wrong. The women weren't necessarily stupid in voting for Trump, especially the wives in the Rust Belt. They want changes, and employment back.'

'Very doubtful they'll get it,' observed Joyce Grimshaw.

'Certainly,' agreed Henry. 'Time will tell.'

'So how did you feel about the result?' asked Mollie, not having seen her neighbour since Wednesday morning.

Henry took a deep breath. He was always uncertain of himself in expressing his politics in front of somebody he did not know, which was the case now with Joyce Grimshaw.

'Exhilarated,' he chanced. Joyce Grimshaw looked hard into the coffee she had just been given by a counter assistant. Henry noticed but carried on as he too took up a cup from the counter.

'I don't know if he will be any good. But it's the old idea of cocking a snook at fashionable wisdom that appeals to me. All their counterparts in America, for instance.' He nodded towards the students at their laptops. 'They've been brought up on political correctness, safe spaces, cultural appropriation, protection of viewpoints and literature running counter to their sensibilities. They must be shell-shocked by the result.'

'I can see that much,' conceded Joyce. 'And I don't necessarily disagree with you. I'm dubious though about the uncharted waters of America having a businessman rather than a politician as president.'

Henry warmed suddenly to his theme. 'Well I have no difficulty with a businessman heading the free world.'

'Really?' questioned Joyce thoughtfully. 'Even one declared bankrupt four times?'

o o o

'Oh certainly, Mollie. She sounds an interesting woman, to have made a complete break from the country after losing her husband like that and starting again in London. Shows some resilience. By all means invite her round here the next time she is staying in Meads.'

Mollie was explaining to Julia about their meeting with Joyce Grimshaw in the morning while Julia had stayed at home to get on with the lunch.

'I'll do that, Julia. She's given me her card. I'll send her an e-mail on Monday.'

Julia was suddenly attentive to the contents of her Scrabble rack. The cogs of her mind began working overtime as she glanced at Henry in an attempt to gauge what his next move would be. He too was deeply absorbed. Despite Mollie's surprising move to let an S go open-ended, he was finding trouble in making use of it. Then he let out an 'Ah!'

'You've found something, Henry,' said Mollie.

'It took a bit of time, and it's not the best use of high-valued letters, but here goes. Perhaps Julia will forgive me.' And so saying, Henry placed on the board SEXY, winning himself twenty-eight points for a double-word score.

Rather than worrying about her sensibilities, Julia was only too relieved that Henry had let alone the open OR staring at her. Having studied the dictionary while Henry was shuffling his tiles around, she was sure of her ground. Proudly she got rid of her rack of seven letters to complete CAPACITOR.

Upon which, and much to Julia's bafflement, Mollie and Henry let out a cry of delight and said in unison to each other: 'Wonder if it's a flux.'

Forgetting her score for the moment, Julia blinked and did not even say 'What are you talking about?' although the question was firmly at the forefront of her mind.

'Sorry, Julia,' said Henry. 'It relates to one of your sister's favourite films, and mine.'

Julia continued to look askance at Henry who was only too enthusiastically ready to explain. 'The flux capacitor is the invention of Doc Emmett Brown to get Marty McFly to go *Back to The Future.*'

Julia placed her head in her hands. 'Oh no,' she exclaimed. 'Not that thing again. Mollie stayed glued to it only last Saturday.'

Mollie laughed. 'Yes, I have to admit, it's never off the small screen and I take every opportunity. There are still one or two scenes I'm not quite word-perfect on.'

Henry laughed again. 'I do appreciate, Julia, it must be irritating for someone not keen on it.'

'That puts it mildly,' scoffed Julia. 'All that nonsense about time travel.'

'Well of course it's nonsense, dear, but it's about more than time travel. The best of science fiction always is.'

Mollie turned to Henry. 'Do you know that the Library theatre is showing it next Thursday in their film season?'

'Yes, I saw the leaflet when it came into the studio. I thought of you immediately.'

Julia looked incredulously at her sister. 'Don't tell me you're going, Mollie.'

'Most certainly. I wouldn't pass up the opportunity to watch it on a large screen.'

Julia rolled her eyes and reached for the bag to draw out another seven tiles.

'Well it had better not be on tomorrow night when *Strictly*'s on. Or I'll have to watch it in my room.'

Mollie exchanged a laugh with Henry. 'Julia's developed a soft spot for Ed Balls.'

'As a matter of fact I have. I couldn't stand him in Parliament. All that smugness and, what do they call it, flat-lining gestures at the Prime Minister. But in this he is showing a vulnerable side. By the way, Henry, did you see Jimmy Young died on Monday?' Julia had a tendency to dart from one name to another.

Henry was distracted on two counts, one of them being his next move. 'Oh yes, he was in his nineties I believe.'

'I loved the various *faux-pas* he could make, and so sagely. Go on, Mollie. Mollie does a wonderful impression of him, being the mimic that she is.'

Mollie rose to the occasion and took a deep breath. 'The pendulum has swung *full* circle, I rather fancy.'

Julia roared with laughter. 'I always liked his programme. I preferred the way he reported what listeners said rather than what happens now, having them on air themselves spouting on. He always kept to the point of what they'd said.'

Henry was frowning in deep thought and mumbled agreement. Then he came to his preoccupation.

'It's short notice, Mollie. But would you come with me on the programme tonight to talk about *Back to The Future*? My arranged interviewee has had to drop out and I'd prefer to fill the space with chat rather than more music. In any case I'd quite like to give the Library theatre a bit of a boost.'

Mollie's face lit up. 'Rather. I always enjoy it.'

'Fine,' said Henry. 'The advantage with hospital radio is that except for a few poor chronic souls, the audience is always different, so we could also chat again about your years as a film extra.'

Mollie clapped her hands with renewed relish, eager to get the Scrabble session out of the way to prepare for the evening.

o o o

'No need to stay, Gerry. I'll lock up.'

The young assistant was glad to get away to a Friday night party and he inched his way out of the cramped studio of Good Health Radio. Henry checked the time and announced: 'Thirty seconds.'

Mollie replaced her headphones and listened as the music came to a stop. Henry turned on his microphone. 'That was the main theme from *Back to The Future*, composed by Alan Silvestri, and played by the City of Prague Philharmonic Orchestra conducted by Nic Raine. Which leads us back into conversation with my guest, Mollie Chadwick. And we'll get on to the film itself in a moment, Mollie. But you were telling us about your fascinating life as a film extra, although you decided to give it up.'

'Yes, I'd had a good life, meeting some interesting people. Not just actors and actresses but technical crew and staff. There was one superb production designer I got to know. He and his wife were especially nice. She was a secretarial assistant. I met them both on *The Mirror Crack'd* in 1980. Lots of crowd scenes in the garden fete and in the house rented by Rock Hudson's character meant lots of work.'

'What prompted you to leave it?'

'The work in general started drying up. It became so spasmodic that I wanted something more definite. Which is how I took up nursing. I was still just about young enough. I decided to go into midwifery if they would have me. I liked the idea of bringing life into the world.'

'How difficult was it to wrench yourself away from film work?'

'In a way I never have. I'm an avid film fan, not so much of the modern films with all their computer graphics. But I still like studying the history of movies. And after going into nursing and then moving down here with my sister, there has been the occasional chance of local work.'

'Such as?'

'Well, for example I spent some time on the Pier working on the last film that David Hemmings made, *Last Orders*. But it started interfering with my nursing so I left it until retirement.'

'And did anything come along after that?'

'A couple of things, yes. There was the remake of *Brighton Rock* a few years ago, again mostly on the

Pier. They couldn't use the Palace Pier at Brighton as it had lost most of its Fifties appearance. The original was of course set in the inter-war years but the new version was taken forward about twenty years. Then there was *Notes on a Scandal* at one of the seafront hotels.' Mollie thought for a moment. 'Oh, and a television Miss Marple, *The Body in the Library*. That was a lot of fun at the Grand Hotel. I could scarcely take my eyes off Joanna Lumley. She had the warmest smile for everybody.'

'She didn't play Miss Marple, did she?'

'Oh no, that was Geraldine McEwan. And it was about the last thing I did. At eighty-five I'm still open to offers, but only if it's in Eastbourne.'

'Well now, as I told our listeners earlier, you are no stranger to us at Good Health Radio. You've done several film reviews for us, although as you mentioned, you are less keen on modern films, unless a classic adaptation comes up, and then you help us out.'

Mollie interrupted her interviewer. 'Up to a point. I have a thing about some adaptations. We mentioned Miss Marple just now. Have you seen what they do to Agatha Christie's work every Christmas? Play around with the plot, put in swear words that would make Dame Agatha turn in her grave, turn parts into black characters who couldn't possibly have been there in the Thirties.'

'I suppose that's seen as dramatic licence,' said Henry, laughing a touch awkwardly.

'Don't you believe it,' said Mollie. 'It's down to a particular faction insisting on making a political statement. Why, have you seen what is happening with a new film about Judy Garland's life? I think they are calling it simply *Judy*'.

'No, what is that?' Henry was somewhat aware that controversy might be looming and he made ready to pull the plug on Mollie if necessary.

'Simply this,' said Mollie getting warmed up. 'Whenever she was in this country, Garland used a British pianist called Burt Rhodes. I ran into him myself once. I was working on a film she made here in 1962 or 63. I'm sure you remember it, Henry, *I Could Go On Singing*.'

Henry said he did.

'Mind you, what a cumbersome title, and based on the daftest of songs. When I think of some of those lyrics: "I could go on singing till the cows come home".' And so saying, Mollie burst out disconcertingly into uncontrollable laughter. Henry had rarely seen her in such exuberant mood and he let her continue for the moment.

'Would have been much better if they'd stuck to the original title, *The Lonely Stage*. Well anyway, hundreds of us were needed to make up the audience in the London Palladium. There were some tense moments there, I can tell you. Her ladyship didn't get on at all well with poor Ronnie Neame who directed the picture. Anyway, Burt Rhodes was there as a musical advisor. The point though was that Burt was a no-nonsense Yorkshireman born in 1923. Can you believe it, in this new film about her, they have actually cast a mixed-race actor to play him? It's absolute *madness*.'

Mollie had raised her voice to such a pitch that Henry decided it was time to rein her in.

'Well, perhaps we'll touch on that subject more broadly another time, Mollie. I want to talk to you about a film that's getting a special showing next week at the Library theatre, because I know it is a favourite of yours. We just heard the theme from it.'

'Ah yes,' said Mollie. '*Back To The Future.*'

'They never stop showing it on television,' continued Henry. 'It seems to have a special place in the repeats schedule, and on so many different channels.'

'Which is fine for us who are devoted to it, and I know you are too. For anyone who isn't, like my sister, it is probably a bore.' Mollie allowed herself an enormous laugh and Henry now sensed that she would be having an infectious effect on his listeners relaxing in bed and tuned in to them. Which reminded him.

'I completely forgot to say,' said Henry, turning up a sheet of paper, 'that we had a request for the theme music, coinciding with our last-minute plan to talk about the film tonight. It was for Gill in Collington Ward. I hope you enjoyed it, Gill. Now then. I know you watch it on television whenever you can, Mollie, but you're still going along to the Library theatre screening next week. Why is that?'

'Oh, because there is nothing like seeing a film on a big screen. I watch it avidly on television as you suggest, but it's not the same.'

Henry had got his guest sufficiently wound up into her subject to plunge on. 'Right now, come on, Mollie. What's the special appeal of the film?'

'Oh, it's the overall warmth, the sense of good over evil. It's a celebration of family life. Think of how concerned Marty is for his future parents when he meets them before he is born.'

'Yes, I want to come back to that aspect. What else?'

'The comedy, both verbal and physical.' Mollie was into her stride. 'Take when Doc Brown asks Marty who the president is in 1985 and Marty tells him Ronald Reagan. Doc is incredulous and queries whether Jerry Lewis is vice-president.'

'Ah yes,' interjected Henry. He knew the answer to his next point but thought some of his audience might not. 'When Doc suggests the First Lady – what a funny title for these days – is Jane Wyman, he gets that wrong, doesn't he? Reagan did marry a film actress but that was Nancy Davis, who of course became Nancy Reagan?'

'No, no,' said Mollie on cue. 'Before he married Nancy, Reagan was indeed married to the *Johnny Belinda* star, Jane Wyman.'

Mollie was clearly on a roll with her movie knowledge and Henry was determined to keep her going. 'You were talking about the verbal comedy. Anything else?'

'Well, I love that scene where Marty sees his criminal uncle as a toddler. The camera is perfectly placed as though in the child's cot before Marty says: "Better get used to those bars, kid." Perfection.'

'You also mentioned physical comedy.'

'Oh yes, that's where Michael J Fox's energy and nimbleness come into their own. When he jumps on to a young boy's scooter, for example, and does everything to get away from the car that Biff is chasing him in, followed by that wonderful cathartic moment. The car crashes into a lorry that dumps its load of manure on Biff and his mates in their open-top car.'

They both laughed at the memory before Henry moved on. 'Is there anything you're unhappy with about the film?'

'Yes, I cringe every time at that moment in the café when Marty is newly-arrived in Hill Valley in 1955. In the phone booth he can't get through to Doc so he tears the whole page out of the directory. That could well have happened in 1985, but never thirty years earlier.'

'I detect this is your interest in the National Campaign for Courtesy coming into its own, Mollie. You've been a member of it for years, I know.'

'Quite so,' said his guest. 'It's not so much that Marty tears the sheet out, although that does deprive anyone else wanting to look up a number. But it's that the café owner sees him do it and doesn't issue a word of recrimination. In 1955 people spoke up always if there was wrong-doing'.

'There could obviously be a sociological study of the film at university level. Perhaps there has been one already. But now I want you to explain something to me, Mollie. It's the one thing I have never understood about *Back to The Future*.'

'What's that?'

'Marty leaves 1985 to go back in time to 1955. At the end he returns to 1985. I can handle all of that. Getting into a DeLorean car, switching on the engine and in thirty seconds he is in the same place thirty years earlier. All perfectly logical. And the reverse process at the end of the film. Fine. I have no problem with the notion of parallel worlds put before me. But how can it possibly be that he goes back to a 1985 life that is very different from the one he left? The family is no longer dysfunctional, their home is much better furnished, and Biff is now subservient to George rather than being his overseer.'

Mollie licked her lips. 'A couple of interpretations there, Henry. One is that in the course of events while Marty is in 1955, a bending of time takes place, rendering it slightly different when he returns.'

'But where is the evidence for that?'

'Well, some see it in the Under The Sea Enchantment Ball when Marty gets his parents together.'

'I'm not convinced, Mollie.' Henry glanced at the studio clock. 'I'm afraid we're going to have to leave your other interpretation for now. But perhaps we can hand it over to our listeners. If any of you are enthusiasts like us of *Back to The Future* and think you have the answer to what is to me a vexed question, then do let us know.'

Henry began winding up *Review Time* by thanking his guest and playing in the show's theme music. Then he adjusted the nightly transfer over to the channel's continuous music loop. The couple got up and left the studio after Henry had switched off and locked up. They made their way through to A & E in order to leave the building through the late-night exit. Friday night meant the inevitable array of drunks who had been brought in with various cuts and bruises. Some of them were rolling about all over the waiting area. Mollie sighed as she and Henry stepped gingerly around them, glad to reach the open air and the walk across to the car park.

'Plenty to talk about, Mollie, if you came back to tell us about the Campaign for Courtesy.'

'You do seem a master of this particular art, Henry,' observed Mollie as she placed her hand on the passenger door handle of his car. I wonder you didn't try your hand at professional broadcasting.'

'Oh I did,' replied Henry. 'This cracked voice of mine was against me.'

'How did you get on with it in the classroom?' Mollie had been dying to put the question for years and only now did it seem natural to ask it. Henry took it head on.

'Funnily enough it never was a problem. Only if I raised my voice, and I never really had to. I saw to it that things didn't reach that stage. It wasn't all that long before I started teaching adults in any case. So there wasn't the problem I had once or twice with children. Somehow I s'pose I managed to get their interest and attention so it was fine.'

'You must have been good at your job,' observed Mollie as she stepped into the car.

'While we're driving home, you can tell me your other interpretation as to why Marty McFly returns to a home in 1985 very different from the one he left.'

Chapter 2a

Al-Jum'ah 10 Safar 1438

Henry Wagstaff looked at the clock. It was about half an hour before he was due downstairs at the sisters' flat. The Scrabble board, bag of tiles and dictionary were ready. No bread pudding this week as Julia had made a cake. Of the two sisters she was the more forceful in declaring that although his bread pudding was first rate, they did not think his cakes were up to scratch. Henry allowed himself a smile at the thought.

It soon left his face as he stared gazing out of his bedroom window at the back of his flat on to the vast communal grounds that nobody felt inclined to maintain any more. He looked again across the lawn to the gap between the houses where he could once see the Congress Theatre, now the Islamic Cultural Centre. His lips tightened as he was reminded of the brush only that morning with the proprietor of the one remaining café in Meads Village.

'It isn't my fault, mate,' he said. 'You know the score. I'd get closed down if I let a woman have a seat in here. I just haven't got the room for a family corner.'

Henry could not argue. He could only look out of the café window at the elderly lady having to stand outside to drink her coffee because of the lack of a segregated area in the establishment. Nearly the middle of November and she looked nipped up with both hands firmly around the coffee cup. It was even worse in the heatwave the previous summer. Women sweltered while having a drink. Henry looked around at the small café. There were plenty of tables empty. But no, this way of life had to obtain at all costs. He was reminded of that by the proprietor as he was only halfway through his coffee.

'Drink up,' the man said. 'We're closing in five minutes for prayers.'

Henry Wagstaff had never come out of the second stage of grief: anger. He tried always to keep it hidden, especially from the sisters who in the Scrabble provided him with the only real diversion of the week. But anger was never far from the surface, even after fifteen years. It was anger that had him insisting with Mollie and Julia that these sessions continue to take place on Fridays, not the Muslim equivalent of Wednesdays. He recalled anew the laugh always created in his classes in Saudi Arabia all those years ago.

'*Anna sa'eed aleum* (I'm happy today).'

'*Leish?* (Why?)'

'*Ashan* al-Arbi'aa (Because it's *Wednesday*).'

The day before the weekend put everyone in a good mood and the lessons that day were a doddle.

Yes, of course it was a small petulant point to make – to insist on perpetuating the western weekend days. It made no real difference to adjust the routine. But control of the traditional Judeo-Christian weekend still stuck in the craw, along with so much else. This though was something one could make a personal stand against. It was why Henry's compassion for the Palestinians was always acute. For the last fifteen years he felt he knew a little of what they had gone through at the hands of the Israelis, just as he, and all of Europe, were going through now at the hands of the Occupiers. It was the perpetual sense of control that did it. He wondered again what had happened to Israel. Nobody ever heard anything about it these days.

Well, they hadn't controlled us three's Friday afternoons, reflected Henry. The sisters had been ready to cave in. Thursday and Friday represent the new weekend, they had said, so we might as well fall in with it. He had admitted to himself that logically they were right. Yet he could not help visualising that shape of the wedge in front of him, and stop himself from staring at the thin end of it.

And so here we were at another eleventh of November. No act of Remembrance at the Eastbourne Memorial in South Street. It seemed far more than fifteen years since anybody had been able to attend one.

Fifteen years! The first stage of grief had certainly kicked in with a vengeance. Denial was indeed the order of that week. You had to hand it to the extremists of the Islamist populations throughout Europe playing their part, ever at the ready. First the Twin Towers in New York. Everyone was taken in wholesale, thinking it exclusively an attack on America. But while all the concentration was on George Bush and his troubles.......

Next had come the news that the House of Saud had fallen in Saudi Arabia and the Wahhabis had taken over, helped by Iraq and Iran. It was still astonishing to think of those two countries joining forces. Before anyone had time to think, the planes went into Big Ben and the Palace of Westminster. After that the Elysée, and all the capitals. The takeover was impressive. They had enough personnel to take on the public services, television stations and governments within hours. They couldn't possibly have managed it without all those already in *situ*. In Britain alone the 20,000 Jihadi suspects on the authorities' radar had stepped up to the plate.

Yet nobody could say we had not asked for it, Henry had claimed. There had been talk of it for years, that Islam would take over Europe. Even his students had said so in Saudi a decade or so earlier. Even they though had probably anticipated a more subtle approach.

Henry sighed and glanced at the clock again. He took one further look at the Islamic Cultural Centre in the distance, left his bedroom, collected the Scrabble things and set off downstairs, where he found that the second stage of grief, anger, was in short supply. A light-heartedness was taking its place. It was a kind of safety valve that despite himself he felt glad of.

'Have you realised what the date is?' offered Henry during the course of the afternoon. He knew neither sister had. They had long given up keeping track of the Gregorian calendar. They relied on Henry and the studied mosque activity for their Fridays. Otherwise it was the weather that kept them up with the seasons. Nor had they minded apparently adapting to it.

When Henry reminded them that today was what they used to refer to as Armistice Day, the room went quiet. Mollie broke the silence. 'When we have tea later, we'll drink to Reggie,' she said in a lowered voice. Julia, who had not known her much older brother, nodded and murmured agreement. It was she who lightened the mood.

'Well, I'll say one thing about this time of year. We would be blasted by now with the commercialism of Christmas if we were still in the old days.'

'Goodness, yes,' echoed Mollie. 'Well into it by now. Do you remember what it was getting to? Starting practically in early September in the shops. The Arndale Centre decorations were up even before Bonfire Night.'

Julia laughed. 'Good lord, yes. Mention of Bonfire Night brings back all those seasonal things; I'd almost forgotten about them. Remember, remember the fifth of November, gunpowder, treason and plot. Then there was Hallowe'en only a few days before it. Must say I don't miss all that trick and treating, nor those enormous bomb-sounding fireworks. But I s'pose it did add some variety to life.'

'It certainly did,' offered Mollie. 'Things always happened to make us aware of the passing of time. A dinner party with friends or a festival such as we've been mentioning. The times we reminded each other, Julia, about a trip to the theatre, trying hard to recall a particular actor's name. Now it's just about getting older, a life mostly of mediocrity, to say nothing of a series of edicts from The Leader.'

Henry kept his cool. He hated this life, but as long as the subject was avoided, he could generally cope. It was when anyone suggested anything approaching advantages to the current way of living that he was in danger of losing his rag. Yet even so, he could not help admitting that when he worked in Saudi Arabia, he did see the benefits the sisters were now espousing about the lack of a run-up to Christmas. He sighed inwardly. How one reacted to the world seemed dependent on choice or lack of it in the matter.

'Can't deny it though. I still miss the annual pantomime.'

'Oh yes, Julia,' echoed her sister. 'I thought I was getting jaded with them, year after year at the Devonshire Park Theatre. Another one of those examples of missing something only when you no longer have it.'

'I still think of the panto we didn't see. Do you remember, Mollie? We had tickets booked months beforehand and were so looking forward to *Aladdin* because it was going to star that young singer and dancer. What was her name? Bonnie Langford.'

'Oh, my goodness, Julia, yes. I'd forgotten about her, a lively effervescent soul. All those artists we used to know. What became of them?'

'And it would have been the first pantomime to be put on by that young chap who'd only just taken over the Theatre.'

'That's right. He'd only been here about a year and had every intention of settling. Came from a theatre in Hertfordshire somewhere. What the Dickens was his name?'

The sisters searched their minds for clues. 'I was always reminded of a middle eastern country as soon as I heard it,' said Mollie. 'Think of middle eastern countries, Henry. You were out there.'

Henry was becoming impatient but he did his social best. 'Qatar? Dubai? Bahrain? Jordan?'

The sisters leaped on the last name and spoke almost in unison. 'Of course, that was it. Jordan. That young chap's name was Chris Jordan.'

A flicker of recognition came over Henry's face. 'Yes, it does ring a bell,' he said, offhandedly.

'Chris Jordan! He came here with a young family. I wonder what ever happened to them all.'

The room went quiet again and Henry made the effort, although by now he had lost the mood. 'Whose turn is it?'

'I think it's mine,' answered Julia, now in deep thought. Mollie murmured confirmation. Julia was relieved that Henry had let alone the open OR staring at her. Having studied the dictionary while Henry was shuffling his tiles about, she was sure of her ground. Proudly she got rid of her rack of seven letters to complete CAPACITOR.

Both Henry and Mollie let out a hollow laugh. 'By heaven, that recalls a memory,' exclaimed Mollie.

'Oh, for you as well, Mollie?' said a somewhat surprised Henry.

'Ah yes. That's if we are both remembering the same thing.' They looked directly at each other and said together 'Flux capacitor,' then burst out laughing. Julia sat bemused, having had the unexpected joy of making an extra fifty points for the deliverance of a seven-letter word wiped away from the occasion.

'Sorry, Julia,' said Mollie. 'That's a terrific word, and by the looks of it a big score.'

'Well, thank you, but it seems to have registered with you two. I don't understand.'

Henry led the way of an explanation. 'It's to do with a film years ago. I was an enthusiast of it and it seems Mollie was too.' Mollie nodded.

'What was it?' asked Julia.

'It was called *Back to the Future*.'

'Oh that thing,' said Julia. 'Yes, I remember you watched it whenever you could, Mollie, until it was banned.'

'That's right, dear. You never liked it while I could never stop watching it.'

'But what has my word got to do with it?'

Henry continued to explain. 'It was the flux capacitor that got the hero, Marty McFly, able to travel back to his hometown thirty years before.'

Julia tossed her head. 'What nonsense!'

Mollie and Henry laughed again. 'It all hinges on that, Julia,' said Henry. 'You have to believe in time travel for the film to make any sense.'

Julia frowned. 'Certainly I couldn't get on with it. But I'm mystified as to why The Leader proscribed it. There was nothing defamatory about Mohammad, no nudity, sex scenes or bad language as far as I recall. What could they have objected to?'

'The Libyans,' said Henry. 'You remember the scene, Mollie?'

'Indeed,' said Mollie. 'They weren't shown in a very good light, were they?'

'Actually they were made to look like idiots, having plutonium stolen from them by Doc Brown. And the shoot-up scene where they came across like Keystone Cops. Our powers-that-be could never have stood for that.'

Mollie and Henry roared with laughter at the memory. Julia prodded Henry to record her newly-won massive score.

Chapter 3

❧

Friday 23 June 2017

'Oh no, Mollie. You've left a triple word score wide open for Henry.'

'Sorry, dear. That's all I could do.'

'Not to worry, Julia,' said Henry, licking his lips. 'I might well be leaving it to you.' His eyes flickered between his tile rack and the board. He looked closely at the D sitting next to the bright red empty triple word score at the bottom edge. But his main gaze was on the A four places above it, next to which was an N. Now if he could fill either side of the resultant open AN, he could shed his seven letters. His mind worked quickly. It always did. There were two double-word scores to mop up too if he could manage it. He also had QU in his rack. Henry's blood pressure was in danger of rising rapidly. His hands shook a little as he shifted the tiles about. He thought he had it, but he needed to check. Picking up the dictionary, he flicked through to the QU's. He shut the OED with a resounding 'Yes!'

'Oh dear,' exclaimed Mollie. 'Henry's found one of his specials.'

Henry tried hard not to look ceremonious as he spread the letters either side of the AN to create

QUITTANCE. When he started counting up the score and went beyond one hundred, Mollie did a mock show of closing her ears.

'There you are, Julia. The triple word is all yours.'

Henry and Mollie knew that Julia would be absorbed for ages working on her new opportunity. And indeed Julia's face became immersed ever deeper in concentration as her head bent further over her rack.

'What about the awful business on Sunday night at Finsbury Park?' said Mollie.

'So hard to imagine the thinking of someone driving a van deliberately into a group of people coming out of a prayer meeting,' observed Henry.

'The only motive seemed to be one of tit-for-tat,' said Mollie.

'Exactly,' answered Henry. 'One of the men attending said on the news next day – did you hear him? – he said: "Why? Why mow down innocent people?" I wonder if he considered that was the question we asked after Westminster Bridge, and then London Bridge.'

'To say nothing of Manchester a month ago,' echoed Mollie. 'When you think of it. Twenty-three mainly young souls perished and another eight hundred wounded.'

Henry reflected. 'Then there was Berlin last Christmas, and Nice a few months earlier. That was another van driven into people, like Finsbury Park.'

'It sounds callous to say it, but only one died there on Sunday night. How many was it in Nice?'

'Over eighty,' replied Henry.

'That's what's so exasperating,' said Mollie, a note of anger rising in her voice. 'They try to make comparisons with these far-right attacks, like Finsbury Park, without realising that they wouldn't happen if it were not for what the extremist Islamists are doing.'

Henry went into his stride. 'Oh, they realise it all right but don't want to admit it. I've been reading a book where the writer talks of Roy Jenkins' part in all this. It appears we've got him to thank for it as much as anybody.'

'How do you mean?' Mollie had one eye on what Julia was doing as she shuffled her tiles around on her rack in between looking earnestly at that triple score waiting to be swallowed up at the foot of the board.

'Well it seems in 1966 when he was Home Secretary....'

'And he did a lot of good,' interrupted Mollie, 'getting homosexuality decriminalised.'

'Oh quite,' said Henry. 'All power to him for that.'

'And frankly for abortion,' returned Mollie. 'Years later when I went into nursing, I heard some hideous stories about back street abortionists.'

'Couldn't agree more,' offered a slightly impatient Henry, irritated by Mollie's interruptions. 'But he was a washout on immigration. It was his determination to launch into cultural diversity – probably the first to use the term – together with, I've remembered the expression, "equal opportunity in an atmosphere of mutual tolerance". Then the book goes on to point out that twenty-five years later, he was musing over the Salman Rushdie affair. You remember the fatwa?'

'Of course.'

'By then he'd become Lord Jenkins and he said in retrospect that we *might* have been more cautious in allowing the creation in the 1950s of what he apparently called substantial Muslim communities here.'

'Oh God, did he really say that?' cried Mollie. 'Thanks a bundle, Roy, for your second thoughts. When left-liberalism gets it wrong with their idealism, they really do screw up, don't they?'

Usually Julia would have winced at such a comment from her sister but she had become too absorbed in her new discovery. 'Oh, I *can* go on the triple,' she exclaimed. 'You've just given me the word in what you were talking about.' And so saying, she placed FATWA along the bottom edge of the board. 'Count it up for me, Henry.'

Henry awarded Julia twenty-seven points, and the board passed on to Mollie.

'What was it you were saying? The Islamist attacks?'

'That's another thing,' said Henry irritably. We've got to be careful now, talking about Islamist attacks rather than Islamic.'

'Yes, and what's the other one? Daesh instead of Isis. I start losing track of it all,' sighed Julia. 'Oh, it all seemed so simple many years ago, when we didn't have all these different foreign influences all around us.'

'Exactly,' said Henry. 'And Roy Jenkins was right when he finally came to his senses if you think of the Suez crisis in '56.'

'Oh yes, that was awful, wasn't it?'

'Sheer madness, Mollie. Considering that Nasser would have taken back control of the Canal only twelve years later anyway. It would have been Egypt's by 1968. Hardly worth the loss of 700 killed in bombing at Port Said.'

'I do agree with you on that one,' said Mollie.

'My parents were never Labour supporters, but they did go to the Albert Hall where Gaitskell addressed the place. They said it was packed out. When you think of it, the opprobrium was every bit as much as there was against Blair over Iraq. Nasser was right when he said Eden had brought the wrath of the whole Arab world down on him. And yet, do you remember, there was not a trace of Islamic terrorism in London or anywhere else.'

'Obviously not,' echoed Mollie. 'We did not have two or three per cent of Arab and Asian Muslims in the population, which a substantial minority of extremists could be taken from. Roy Jenkins never lived to see the fruits of that in later years.'

'Mind you,' said Julia. 'I couldn't help being struck by what that woman said on *Question Time* last night.'

Henry said he had missed it.

'They were arguing the toss about people's attitudes to immigration.'

'That's right,' interjected Mollie, looking up from her tile rack. She's a bigwig I believe in the Green Party. I quite liked her.' She returned to concentrating on the matter in hand.

Julia continued. 'The woman accepted that most people thought the rate of immigration was too high. But she said another survey showed a similar majority was happy with the ethnic minority people they knew personally or living next door to them.'

'I see no contradiction in that,' claimed Henry. 'It's what Desmond Morris wrote about years ago. Do you remember his book, *The Naked Ape*?'

Mollie was abstracted. 'Vaguely. I never read it.'

'I remember the gist of it. If a foreigner joins a circle of ten natives, he's feted. Two foreigners will be tolerated, but three will be rejected. History is littered with examples of what happens when cultures are forced together. The Balkans and Caucasus have provided rich evidence. As for Africa, where do you start?'

'Except don't forget with Africa, that was the colonial powers carving up the continent and drawing straight lines across it.'

'I quite agree with you, Mollie, and then so many tribes were mixed up that hadn't been before. But that is just my point.'

Henry could not help noticing that his friends were losing the thread. He tried another tack.

'I like people I know and I reckon I'm fairly gregarious. But on the odd occasion I can't avoid going up to London, it's a different matter. When I get off the train and step on to the concourse at Victoria, and am nearly knocked sideways by the mobs, especially those who rush into me with their heads buried in their mobile phones, then my attitude to people changes rapidly.'

Mollie laughed. Her concentration on Henry was beginning to return. 'Why do you avoid London, Henry?'

'That's part of it, what I've just said. The crowds and the rush. And because of so much foreign influence. If I take the 148 to Lancaster Gate a couple of times a year to visit an old friend, often I don't hear a word of English on the bus, except for when I get off and say thank you to the driver – who looks at me as though I'm mad. The place is no longer representative of the country it's supposed to be the capital of.' Henry was beginning to look red in the face.

'I don't know,' said Mollie, attempting a last reshuffle of her tiles before settling on her final decision. 'I would miss our trips up to the National for the matinees Julia and I go to.'

'Fine,' said Henry. 'The art galleries, museums and so on. But for the rest, you can keep the place. When I think of what's happened to my old stamping ground where I taught for a while.'

Julia laughed. 'You taught in so many places, Henry. Where was this?'

'Newham,' replied Henry. 'Two to three years teaching immigrant youngsters English. Which is why I don't disagree with the woman on the programme. I got a kick out of getting those kids to be able to converse and get on with their ordinary lessons. I enjoyed knowing their parents too. They were all co-operative, even though communication with them was often difficult.

'But there was still an Englishness central to the place in the late Seventies. The large café opposite the school was run by a group of Cockney women. Along High Street North there were shops like Arthy's Bakery, run for years by traditional Londoners. Between there and Ilford, where I was based, the brother of Brian Poole of the Tremeloes, you remember them?' The sisters nodded. 'Arthur Poole had his butcher's shop on Romford Road. Now look at the place. A full 73% of Newham comprises ethnic minority people. None of the indigenous folk asked for that.'

'Yes, that's it, isn't it? said Mollie. 'Old Lord Roy Jenkins if he was still alive would have a lot to answer for. Like his modern-day counterparts. Sadiq Khan goes on about London being the most cosmopolitan capital in the world, as though that's what people want, those whose families have lived there for generations.'

Henry warmed to his theme. 'I'm clear in my own mind. I want to carry on living my life immersed in my own culture, with all its foibles and faults as well as its pleasures. And not in a melting pot of other people's cultures, no matter how good that's reckoned to be for us.'

'Well stay in Eastbourne, Henry. Apart from a few.....'

'Which I don't mind at all,' interjected Henry. 'I wouldn't want to lose our doctor. Shefik al Katatni's a brilliant man.'

'Exactly. But apart from a few, there won't be much chance of our traditional culture being overturned here. Nor, thank God, much chance of Islamist outrages.'

'I wish I could share your optimism,' said Henry. 'After all these attacks by vans ramming into crowds, have you seen the new steel bollards strung out along the pavement in front of the Winter Garden?'

Julia's eyes opened wide. 'Is *that* what they're there for?'

Henry nodded grimly. 'Not that you'd get a straight answer from the Council about it. A chap I know asked point blank for the reason they've been put there. Do you know what their answer was?'

The sisters shook their heads.

Henry adopted an authoritative air. 'The bollards are a security feature called a Hostile Vehicle Mitigation (HVM) measure that was recommended by the Police as part of the Devonshire Park redevelopment project.'

The sisters burst out laughing and Mollie saw her opportunity in the softened mood. 'Here we are. Done it.' Using the E left open, she placed on the board GLADE. 'It's on a double-word that makes up twenty-eight. If I'd added an S, that would have given me two more points but it didn't seem worth it.'

'Very wise not to waste an S. But now we know,' offered Henry, winking at Julia. 'Mollie's got an S to spare.'

'Oh damn,' cried Mollie, annoyed at her disclosure.

All three laughed and Henry asked the sisters about plans for Mollie's birthday the following day.

'And that's another sobering thought,' she said. 'It's a year today since the Referendum. We haven't got very far with it, have we?'

'Certainly not after the Election,' observed Henry. 'Mrs May losing her majority like that; it's put us even further back. What is it with these politicians? "Nothing has changed", she said. Everything has. The Tory rebels have got her firmly by the windpipe. Who knows when we'll leave the European Union now?'

Mollie nodded wistfully.

'Might all be academic anyway,' laughed Henry, 'when you think of what Gaddafi said the year before he was seen off, insisting Europe's future was Islamic. Mind you, I read recently his speech about it was made in Rome to five hundred young women, each one paid seventy euros to listen to him. Clown!'

Chapter 3a

❦

Al-Jum'ah 28 Ramadan 1438

For once Julia was on a roll. Although it had happened once or twice, seldom did she place a seven-letter word on the board. The last time had been 10 Safar the previous year. Despite their competitive spirit, both Mollie and Henry were pleased for her. In fact it had been Henry who had helped her. As usual he preceded Julia's turn and during the one he had just taken, she'd held her breath lest he take away the opportunity she saw looming. It all depended on whether he had an S to get rid of. He might have; she glanced over the board to find no others laid down. Henry pondered longer than usual, then sighed as all he could muster was a miserable LONE. He always preferred to bite the bullet with what he had rather than pick up another seven letters from the bag, throw a bad deal back and lose a turn.

Julia's excitement mounted. On another part of the board altogether, she placed, with somewhat shaking hands, the word SAGGING, one of the G's represented by a blank tile. She could not hide her glee as she announced what she had worked out, and gone over three times: a total score of seventy points.

'Well done, Julia, even though you have taken away the chance I had of placing my own S.' Mollie laughed good-naturedly as she said it.

Buoyed by her success, Julia almost skipped out to the kitchen to make the tea. The threesome spent the next half an hour in good spirits. They were even light-hearted about the latest edict from the local representative of The Leader. The piercing cry of *Allahu Akbhar* over the loudspeakers at the end of Chessington Gardens also passed them by. The call to prayer usually did now, coming at them several times a day. However, the sound did spark off a thought in Mollie's mind.

'Do you ever have any nagging concerns about your own departure from Saudi Arabia, Henry, in terms of our present life?'

'Not now,' he replied. 'It happened such a long time ago. If they were going to take any action, they'd have done it years ago. It was on my mind for the first year or two, but not after that. In any case the Saudis were never aware of it. Aeronautics UK were anxious to get rid of me before the Saudis could get their hands on the article. They needed to save their own skins.'

'I hope you're right,' laughed Mollie. 'What would we do without you on Friday afternoons if you were carted away?'

They laughed and waited for Julia to return with the tea trolley. She was eager to get on with the second game to see if her luck could continue. In fact lightning did strike twice. Fairly early on she was able to place on the board LUNCHES, with the help of another blank letter. It was on a triple word score, awarding her ninety-eight points. The others never caught up with her, mainly because their second game never came to an end.

As he was musing over his next move, Henry said, almost abstractedly: 'I sometimes wonder if I'd have felt the same about Saudi if the invasion here had not happened. Now of course I regret ever going out there. But I had eleven years back here before they took over. Yet while I was out there, I never had any regrets about being there. Not that I recall anyway. But I knew what was going on around me, just as we know it now. The constant sense of oppression; never saying a word against Islam; men and women always segregated.'

'Well, you weren't directly affected by it then, were you? Not like now.' This from Mollie.

Henry sighed. 'That's the power of money, I suppose. Just the same now. All the riches flowing from the ground. Over there we used to talk about petrodollars oozing out. Now it's shale gas riyals. Nobody paying taxes, salaries skyrocketing. Look at our pensions, tripling overnight. All that keeps a lot of people quiet.'

'Meanwhile what happens to the environment?' sighed Mollie. 'Not a whisper in years since they mowed down all the protesters at Balcombe. Must have been the same all over the country, but we've never heard a word about it.'

'Strange isn't it?' mused Henry. 'Just how much can be accepted when money is involved. And looking back, that's exactly how it must have been with me when I worked out there.'

'Come on, you two,' exclaimed an exasperated Julia, itching to get on with the game she was winning.'

'Yes, sorry, it's my turn,' said Mollie. She pondered a while longer. 'My God, that character was right in one of our favourite plays.' She glanced at her sister. 'Do you remember, Julia? *Waters of the Moon*? What was his name who said: "The human animal is very adaptable"?'

'Winterhalter,' answered Julia, leaning down over her Scrabble rack. 'Julius Winterhalter.'

'That's him. When you think of the atrocities that go on now. We'd never have accepted them before.'

'Like this morning's episode,' observed Henry, repositioning several tiles. 'That's what got me thinking all this again. The young man thrown off the Correction Tower for being homosexual.'

The room froze in the sudden silence, until Henry broke it again. 'There were always rumours that was happening when I was in Saudi nearly thirty years ago. We never knew if they had any substance and we never discussed it much. Just thought that if it was true, it was their culture, so let them get on with it. One or two of them, the artisans, or the heavies as we called them, even joked about poufters being given flying lessons. Mind you, that's what they thought all of us teachers and even technical instructors were.' Henry laughed grimly. 'Reckoned all of us were nancy boys.'

Mollie spoke quietly and noticed that her sister had started shaking. 'Do we know who was executed?'

'Apparently a Philippino servant lad. I happened to be walking along the corniche about an hour later. There were people about, one or two had just arrived on the scene. They'd been pulled in to watch the proceedings. You know what it's like for people who happen to be close by.'

'Can't you call it the seafront?' Julia's voice was shaking out of control.

'Sorry, Julia,' said Henry, exchanging a glance with Mollie. 'It's just that people call it the corniche now.

Anyway, the talk around was that the boy hadn't acted with discretion and he was caught. He must have behaved way off the radar. There was enough risk taken in my time out there. I was kerb-crawled no end of times walking through the streets of Al Khobar.'

Suddenly Julia burst into tears. Mollie got up so quickly that her Scrabble rack and tiles scattered. She placed her arms around her sister's shoulders but the weeping continued.

Henry got up too. 'I've still got some brandy hidden upstairs. I opened it about a year ago, so it should still be all right. I'll go and get it.' He disappeared hurriedly.

Mollie sat down again, still holding on to her sister. 'Try and calm yourself, dear. We know these dreadful things go on sometimes. We're back where we were throughout the 1930s and beyond until the law was changed. Most of the gays have gone to ground again. There's not a thing we can do in these times.'

Julia whimpered. 'I was a part of it. I was a part of it.'

Mollie released her hands for a moment. 'What do you mean, dear?'

'I was as bad as anybody. I hated homosexuals.'

'I'm sure you don't mean that, Julia. There was an atmosphere against them. We were all brought up to believe it was wrong. We all made jokes about them, calling them queers and shirt-lifters and all the rest of it. The police acted on what the people themselves thought about them. I recall vividly Mother once saying they should all be chucked in the canal. We were all conditioned. You were only going along with the herd, as we all did.'

'No, no,' cried Julia. 'My feelings were of utter contempt, hatred.'

'You kept this so quiet. But why, Julia? Why did you feel so intensely about it?'

Julia settled for a moment, wiping her nose. 'I never told anybody. I was sixteen, just started in the shipping office. Never much sure of myself in those days, travelling up to Cheapside every day. There was an uproar about a group of men caught together in a club off St Martin's Lane. It was in all the papers. A couple of lawyers, actors, people like that. They were all sent to prison. The girls in the typing pool were all talking about it. I didn't have a clue what it all meant. One lunch time I sat with my best friend eating our sandwiches on a bench in St Paul's Churchyard. I've never forgotten it. Jenny was older and knew much more than me about everything. I asked her straight out what it was that men did together that was so bad.

'She was very explicit. I felt so sickened I couldn't eat any more lunch. I never felt so disgusted in my life. I thought men who could do that with each other were pure *evil*.'

Mollie sat back in her chair and thought for a moment before answering her sister. 'Oh, Julia, I suppose it can seem so complicated at times. Thinking back I felt the same as you when I first realised what men did to have sex together, until I started meeting couples on the film sets and could see how much they loved each other. And they did, in a way that put many a straight couple to shame. I could see that their view of making love, or even of having straightforward sex, was so different from ours. I began to see it didn't make them wrong and us right, necessarily. It was something they didn't only enjoy; they thrived on it. It breathed life into them.'

Mollie got up and poured out some tea still in the pot. 'Here, drink this. Henry's probably having trouble finding the brandy.'

She continued. 'In these subjugated times of course we haven't heard of a gay political lobby for years. But I always thought they were their own worst enemies. Perhaps you couldn't blame them; they had a lot of ground to make up. But it was clear to me when I took up nursing, studying anatomy and all that. Many straight men were physically nauseated, as you were, by gay activity. That wasn't repression or prejudice or even homophobia, but a literal gut reaction. I always thought that was something the gay pressure groups never even began to address. Always harping on about their rights and nothing else. Same with all the Pride business. Remember that? Heavens, that seems an age ago now. They had no reason to be *proud* of their sexuality, any more than ashamed of it. I always felt pride was about doing things, achieving things, not about being anything. *You* might as well be proud of being left-handed.'

Mollie put down the teapot. 'There were times when I found the whole thing tiresome. And I once had my own demons tested to the limit.'

Julia looked up at her as she wiped her tears away. Mollie sat down again.

'Yes, I had one particularly difficult time. I've never told you about this either. Not long after Mother died, it was. I was working on *Oh, What a Lovely War* down at Brighton. It must have been 1968. Dickie Attenborough wanted some lively crowd scenes on the old West Pier. We were all geared up in Edwardian costumes.'

'I remember that,' Julia cut in. 'You invited Father down for the day to watch.'

'That's right. I knew we were wanted only for the morning. I asked Dad to come down and see what was going on and then I could spend the afternoon with him before he took the train back.' She got up to look out of the window. 'He was enjoying himself tremendously, and I really got the impression he was taking his mind off losing Mother, just for a while anyway.'

She paused and Julia waited for her to go on. 'What happened?'

Mollie sighed. 'We were having a general wander, and came back to Old Steine. Dad was suddenly in need of a lavatory. You remember how he was with his prostate trouble?'

Julia nodded.

'Well, he was so desperate that I pointed him in the direction of a particular loo. It was the only one close by. But I was immediately apprehensive. I knew it was a place where men loitered to pick each other up, and solicited for others.'

'Oh God, 'said Julia. 'I think I know what you're going to say.'

Mollie looked back from the window. She nodded. 'When Dad came out of that place, he looked awful, upset, awkward, confused. He'd probably never experienced anything like that. He didn't say anything of course. He didn't need to. But I was so bloody angry, Julia. By that time it didn't matter to me what men did together. But how dare they inflict their needs on those who didn't feel the way they did? What right, I thought, did they have to impinge on the privacy of men who were only needing a public convenience for the purpose it was intended for?'

Julia looked unhappy for Mollie.

'I couldn't get it out of my head the rest of the day. And Dad, feeling so raw at the time for the loss of Mother, clearly didn't get over it either. After that I had no time for any excuses that were ever made for this cottaging as they called it. Of course, since the Occupation, we've never heard of it. And no wonder, given what happened to that poor wretched boy today.'

Mollie returned to gazing out of the window. 'That was the trouble in those days, when we had a Left, especially with the young led by university students. If you didn't accept and embrace any liberal reform in every particular, they considered you were against them.'

She turned back from the window. 'Mark you, I'd give anything to have them back, and the arguments with them all over again. Anything rather than this sterility, devoid of theatre and cinema, ideas and discussion.'

Julia appeared to be calming down. She remained quiet for a moment. 'I still don't understand it, Mollie,' she said quietly as she sipped more of her tea. 'But I do feel terrible about what happened to that boy this morning.'

'Of course you do, Julia. And I do too. It was the action of medieval primitives, which this regime is all about and no two ways about it. Probably we won't see it in our lifetimes, but it will come to an end. Bad times have a habit of doing that.'

They heard movement on the stairs. 'Henry must have found that brandy.'

Chapter 4

✿

Friday 13 July 2018

'This was the scene of one of my crimes. The unfortunate thing is that it looks so different now. It was all filmed before the fire.'

'Yes, that was a sad thing indeed,' said Joyce Grimshaw. 'I remember vividly seeing the pictures on television.' Then she laughed. 'And of Cameron and Osborne down here days later, as another election was looming.'

The sisters were walking abreast with Henry Wagstaff and Joyce along the wide central section of Eastbourne Pier. Joyce was on one of her Eastbourne breaks staying at her Meads guest house. The three residents of the town noticed how she was taking deep breaths while she had the opportunity.

'I wouldn't change living in Battersea for anything now, but oh, what a joy to come down here for the sea air.'

'Just for the weekend?' asked Henry.

'No, I'm staying until Wednesday.'

'That's good,' said Julia. 'Perhaps we can meet up again to go out to Alfriston. The bus service is getting pared down all the time but we could work round the timetable somehow.'

'No need,' said Henry. 'I'll run us out there one day next week. Morning coffee or lunch or whatever. Then we can have a look at the smallest church in England.'

'Oh, is that Lullington?' queried Joyce. 'I've always wanted to see that.'

'That's settled then. We'll sort out a day.'

'Tell me more about the filming here, Mollie.'

'It was about five or six years ago. There was this lovely old domed building on the deck area where we're walking now, that went down in the fire. But the crowd work was as much on the beach. Let's walk across.'

Mollie led the group over to the pier railing with a view across to Hastings and Fairlight Cliffs in the far distance. The day was brilliantly sunny and the sea sparkled. She pointed down to the beach immediately close to the Pier.

'There was a huge crowd of us jostling around while poor Phil Davis was meeting his end right underneath here.'

'I didn't see the latter version of *Brighton Rock*, but I'll have to look for the DVD now. You've got me interested in it.'

'Personally I didn't think it measured up to the original. Nobody could've beaten the young Attenborough in the 1947 version. But it was fun and there were some good moments. I preferred Helen Mirren in our version to Hermione Baddeley in the first.'

'You'll have realised, Joyce, that Mollie is quite an aficionado on films.'

'Too true, Julia. I had gathered that from other visits.'

The group of four laughed good-naturedly.

'I'm glad Mollie and Henry met you a year or two ago. We do enjoy meeting up with you when you come down here.'

'It's nice for me too. I always like coming here. Now I feel I have got connections. And for once I'm not sorry to be away from London, while Trump is here.'

Henry smiled to himself as they started walking towards the Edwardian tea rooms in the centre of the Pier. The president had touched down at Stansted the previous afternoon, causing mayhem in London.

'It has certainly given rise to a lot of hypocrisy with the virtue-signallers,' voiced Henry.

'How so?' Joyce stiffened. The others noticed.

'Don't get me wrong, Joyce.' Henry immediately tried to placate their friend and visitor. 'I have no illusions about Trump now. I don't know that I ever did. But there really is a lot of hypocrisy spouted about the man compared with others.'

'I have to agree with that,' piped up Mollie. 'I thought the same especially after spotting an article in *The Guardian* this week.'

'Have you been reading *The Guardian* again, Mollie?' Julia's tone was enough to make Mollie feel as though her hand had been caught in the biscuit barrel.

'Well, only when I'm in town and browse in the library. Then I have a glance or two at the newspapers in general. No bad thing to look at other viewpoints, surely.'

'I thought that was why you were so insistent on our subscribing to *The Week*.'

Joyce saw her chance to come in. 'You mean you can overdo these things, Julia? Just for the record, I take *The Guardian* every day.'

Julia managed a half smile but did not welcome what she saw as a smirk on Joyce's face. 'Well what was this article you saw, Mollie?'

By then the group had reached the door of the tearooms, which Henry held open as they walked in.

'It's this chap who writes for the paper, Owen Jones. He was banging on about the protests against Trump, but all the time I was reading what he said, I wondered what kind of protest he'd helped organise against Xi Jinping of China, or Jacob Zuma of South Africa, who was awarded a State Visit, which they're talking about giving Trump.'

'It's double standards again, Mollie,' said Henry. 'You can't get away from them.'

'It's all the more maddening when it comes from someone so very young and self-regarding as Owen Jones,' said Mollie, 'all of which is a pity as the boy is so dishy.'

'What, Owen Jones?' queried Henry.

'Yes, Henry, very dishy.'

Henry laughed and suggested they aim for one of the remaining window tables looking towards Beachy Head.

'That looks wonderful,' said Joyce, sitting down, absorbed in the view. 'Incidentally, Mollie, I agree with you entirely about Owen Jones. The boy is drop-dead gorgeous.'

The foursome laughed, even Julia allowing herself a slight smile. Then they nattered over the menu, deciding variously on coffee only or accompanied by toasted teacakes. A waitress was by their side within minutes and they made their collective order.

'Oh, this is nice,' said a relaxed Joyce, as she watched the waitress disappear towards the kitchen. 'I can just imagine this scene exactly the same a hundred years ago. Not even any blaring music in here that you often get.'

'Yes, and it probably looks pretty much the same in demographic terms as well.'

'I suppose it is,' Joyce agreed. 'I see a quite different picture in Battersea, which is fine by me. But unlike the impression we're all given, most places in England, and certainly villages, will not have altered much in that respect now.'

'Exactly so, Joyce,' said Henry. 'What about this idiot of a TV journalist? Did you see what he wrote this week about the area he'd been in, in Derbyshire? Talked about a "worryingly white" village. He'd find the same in most. You look at any documentary about English villages. Penelope Keith's series, for instance, about the best-kept village. The cameras go into group gatherings, village fetes and the like, and you'd be hard pressed to find any black or brown faces. Or the vet programmes up and down the country. With about 80% of us not multi-anything, what else do they expect? And when I think of my time out in northern Zambia, I dread to imagine what would happen if somebody wrote in the *Times of Zambia* that the Northern Province was worryingly black.'

'You're right,' put in Mollie. 'It was like that nonsense over the *Midsomer Murders* producer. I worked a couple of them myself. The poor chap got the push because of his answer to the query about why there weren't more black faces in the cast. He said straightforwardly because there were scarcely any black people living in the areas depicted.'

Henry looked aghast. 'Did that really happen?'

'Yes,' confirmed Mollie. 'Even though I recall vividly being part of a law court scene where the prosecuting counsel, quite authentically, was black.'

'Do you know, I always wondered if that was the reason they got rid of *Heartbeat*, because it was essentially monocultural.'

'Oh, I wouldn't be at all surprised. And that leads to one of my bugbears: colour-blind casting,' answered Mollie.

'Yes, this does get to you, doesn't it? You mentioned it the last time you were on *Review Time* with me.'

'Indeed, and what I find so annoying is the lack of consistency. They cast ethnic minority people in obviously white parts while there's the hell to pay if they try the reverse. There was the case of a theatre in your old stamping ground, Henry, the Hackney Empire.'

Henry laughed. 'Oh, good lord, that was the first theatre I ever went into as a kid. What's happened there then?'

'A Welsh company was booked in for their tour of the Chinese play, *The Golden Dragon*. Then the powers-that-be turned it down, on the grounds that the actors were white British and not Asian.'

Henry tossed his head impatiently.

'We do see this from time to time at the Devonshire Park,' said Julia. 'Even in *The Importance of Being Earnest*, one of our favourites, they had a black man playing Rev Chasuble. He was very good and warm in the part, but in the 1890s, he wouldn't have been that colour, and finishing up marrying an elderly spinster like Miss Prism.'

'We're not supposed to notice things like that these days,' offered Mollie.

The waitress arrived and distributed coffee and teacakes as directed. Henry asked for the bill. As she left the group a flurry of protests about payment ensued until Henry insisted on treating them. Mollie started to pour out the coffee.

'You have a point when it comes to consistency,' agreed Joyce. 'But I truly cannot understand your thinking, Henry, about mixed cultures in a society. After all, you just said you worked in Zambia. It seems it was all right for *you* to go to another country. What's the difference?'

'Every difference,' answered Henry, who had received the same challenge a number of times. 'Both in Africa, and in the Middle East, I was in the respective territories for as long as the authorities wanted me there, not the other way around. I didn't have *carte blanche*, and rightly so, to throw my culture about as in the old colonial days, much less to have public funds spent on its perpetuation, as is the case here constantly.'

'But, Henry,' persisted Joyce. 'I love the life I live in Battersea, around the village on Sunday mornings having late breakfast sitting outside one of the many bistros, meeting people from many cultures. I wouldn't go back to Shropshire for anything.'

'But that's just the point, Joyce,' said Henry. 'For you it was a matter of choice. It wasn't for us living in Hackney. The cinemas, the Empire that Mollie just mentioned. Of course some of these things come to a natural end. But everywhere there was a rich Cockney atmosphere. Everyone understood everyone's common culture. It was all turned upside down within a space of twenty years, without the population of generations past having any say in it. By contrast it was your choice to leave Shropshire and move into the sort of society you wanted.'

'Nevertheless, we are a multicultural society now,' offered Joyce.

'And there's a massive problem with that assertion. Many millions of people never asked for, and I am convinced, never wanted a multicultural society in the first place. With the result that twenty, thirty years down the road, or however long it's been, continuing millions of people, often the same ones, given age longevity, are persistently told to accept something that was forced on them from the beginning. That is a very shaky psychological stance from which to operate.'

Joyce paused for a moment. 'But Henry. Why are you so opposed to multiculturalism?'

'Because with its inception, it presupposes no further recognition of a host-nation culture, into which all other cultures are prepared to absorb themselves, their citizens having made the conscious decision at one generational stage or another to settle in it.'

Joyce thought for a moment. 'You do seem bound up with the idea of a host-nation culture.'

'Yes, I am, Joyce. A healthy sense of national identity is a prerequisite for a thriving and just society. What the Left still fails to understand is that so-called right-wing populism is not an expression of national identity; it results from a crisis *in* national identity. And I'll give you an example, of my time teaching in Newham. The head teacher told me of the parent she'd had to pacify that morning. She was Jewish and she spoke passionately of how her family had come over from Austria in the Thirties and had done everything they could to mould themselves into the life they'd adopted in the east end of

London, even against the antisemitic odds of the time. And what were they seeing now? Ethnic minorities being encouraged to regard their cultures as equal and not be bothered about absorbing themselves into the society they had found here.'

Henry was getting into his stride. 'And make no mistake. It wasn't the ethnic people themselves making the running. I saw that myself in Stratford and Forest Gate. It was all the do-gooding whites who felt the need to put their oar in. All of them Labour supporters like you probably.'

Silence descended on the group and an icy tension took over suddenly. Mollie and Julia exchanged an embarrassed glance. Then Joyce spoke softly. 'Please don't make that kind of assumption, Henry. If you must know, I hover between the Lib Dems and the Greens, with no allegiance to either.'

'I'm sorry, Joyce.' Henry lowered his voice. 'I don't know what came over me.'

Joyce laughed and the tension broke. 'That's all right. I'm sure we can have a civilised discussion, even an argument, without getting into a stew. But I do ask you, Henry, to acknowledge the good that has come from the mix of different peoples in this country.'

'Depends which way you look at it.'

'I really don't think it does, you know. All the fashions, the foods, so much that has been introduced to us.'

'Yes, well I've always thought that was overdone. One of my favourite dishes is curry. I cook a lot of it: chicken, beef, veg. But I don't need half a dozen Bangladeshis in my kitchen looking over my shoulder as I'm preparing it.'

Joyce joined in with the laughter that ensued from Henry's observation.

'But it's not just that,' he continued. 'One of the things I find so tiresome is the idea that multiculturalism has been one long success story. Bit like the treasurer of a local society who presents his balance sheet at the AGM and gives an account only of the income; nothing about the expenditure.'

Joyce looked faintly bemused. 'What expenditure in this case?'

Henry pursed his lips before answering, determined to collect the thoughts together that had shaped his thinking. 'Well, for a few examples, before we had multiculturalism introduced into our society, we did not have honour killings, enforced marriages, female genital mutilation, modern slavery and human trafficking, an exponential increase in gang warfare and knife crime, localised sharia law. Nor did we have the constant risk of suicide terrorist attack, still regarded by the security authorities as substantial. We had none of that before multiculturalism was inflicted on our – and yes, I will say it again, Joyce – our host-nation culture.'

Henry sat back, breathing hard.

Mollie looked awkwardly around the table. 'More coffee, anybody?'

Chapter 4a

Al-Jum'ah 29 Shawwal 1439

'Come on, Julia. Let me fix it or we'll be late for the bus.'

'No rush, Mollie. They are every twenty minutes after all.' Julia was always agitated about fixing her niqab in place, even after all the years of practice. Mollie had got hers on, a mass of blackness, a shroud over the whole of her body with only the slit for eyes to peep through.

'No, dear, it's Friday. The buses are every hour.'

'Oh yes, of course. I forgot.'

Mollie adjusted Julia's identical garb and they started their descent of the staircase like a couple of awkward penguins. Julia was always hindered by the covering clouding her eyesight as her glasses never failed to steam up with it on while she was indoors. Which was why Mollie always led the way down the stairs in case Julia lost her footing. They reached the front door and let themselves out. Julia breathed a sigh of relief as they stepped out along the front path to the pavement and turned left to make for the bus stop opposite the back of the Ramada Hotel in Compton Street.

As Julia slid her arm through her sister's, Mollie waited for the usual observation. She was not disappointed. 'That's better. My specs do seem to clear as soon as I'm out in the open. I don't know how surgeons get on who wear glasses over their masks. How can they see through them to make their incisions?'

Mollie sighed. Stage four of grief was depression and Mollie recalled no end of it in the early days, much of it in dealing with Julia. Now that she had reached the stage of merely going over her views repeatedly, Mollie could cope with that. They turned the corner and saw a small queue of women ahead. This July day was already warm and the sisters were starting to sweat under their regulation clothes.

'Oh lord,' observed Julia. 'A lot of women today, and we won't all get on our section. Glory, there's the dreadful Mrs Johnson. At least the niqabs conceal our identities; you can say that about them.'

'Hardly, Julia. If we recognise Mrs Johnson despite what she's wearing, the same must be true of us, especially arm-in-arm.' Mollie had ceased to find it tiresome in making the same point to Julia.

Instinctively Julia let go of Mollie's arm. They joined the back of the queue just as the single-decker bus turned the corner from Silverdale Road towards them. As predicted, space was at a premium and the usual commotion started. A man got on first and went straight into the front section of the bus. He was the only one there. The first two women showed their passes to the driver, stepped off again and walked to the back entrance to climb into the women's section, which was already full.

'Sorry, ladies,' the driver announced to the rest of the group. 'No more room.'

'This is ridiculous,' said the strident Mrs Johnson. 'You've got all this space for male passengers and hardly anybody in it. But the much smaller area for women is always full. Can't you be a bit imaginative and change the areas around if you must separate us?'

The driver sighed. It was the same old argument in this area of Eastbourne and its ratio of women to men. He sympathised with the ladies and what they were saying made sense. But he had his instructions. 'You know exactly what it's like. If I did make the change, sensible though it is, and one of the RBIs got on, I'd be in trouble.'

Mollie was always bemused by the description of the RBIs: the religious bus inspectors. Inspectors they certainly were, but religious? The group knew though that the driver was right and they sighed deeply. Most of them stood back to wait for the next bus. The sisters did not.

'Well, you can avoid Mrs Johnson now,' observed Mollie as they began stepping out to the town centre and the Eastbourne Souk. To her surprise, Julia asked if they could go via the corniche.

'Yes, if you want to, I'm certainly game for a sea front walk. We'll have to watch the time. It's Friday so the shops will be shut from noon, remember.'

Julia tut-tutted. 'I do keep forgetting this is like Sunday, isn't it? Those women will have to wait another hour for the bus as you said.'

'Some of them wouldn't be able to walk so they've no choice. In any case we've got Henry for Scrabble this afternoon, so we don't want to be too late getting lunch and clearing up.'

By then they were almost on to the Western Lawns and turning left.

'Let's stay this side of the road, Mollie.'

'Yes, of course.' Mollie knew what was in Julia's mind. Neither of them wanted to be drawn in if there was a punishment about to take place in the old bandstand ground. Thankfully they did not often occur in Eastbourne, perhaps one execution a year. But they had been caught once in the early days, pushed into watching the events in Chopping Square as it was now called. It took them years to come to terms with what they had witnessed. And sure enough, they saw a crowd ahead of them, some of them shouting. The noise grew. The worst of it for the sisters was the knowledge that it was often their own people baying for the blood of a murderer.

They had no need to say anything to each other. Julia was holding Mollie's arm again as they reached Lascelles Terrace and turned sharply into it to get away from the corniche. They hurried down the road and were relieved to find the comparative safety of the junction of Chiswick Place and the Devonshire Park Mosque. They always tried hard not to look at the building, the memories of their happy evenings when it was a theatre too painful, even now.

They made their way along Chiswick Place into Cornfield Road and slowed their pace. The thoughts of what was going on at the old bandstand and the increasing heat of the day was making them perspire even more under their niqabs. It was time to switch off again, a process that had become remarkably easy to them, just to relax and go with the flow of life. There was no alternative if one discounted suicide.

They reached the Souk and walked inside. At least the air-conditioning was on full blast, which kept Julia's glasses from steaming up. Perversely they were now glad of their restricting garb as they would otherwise shiver under the blast of cold air. As always, they marvelled at the sights they saw, so different from when it used to be the Arndale Centre. Henry had told them the Souk was a copy of those he used to know in Saudi. Every other shop was full of gold. It could afford to be. With so much money sloshing around, people seemed able to buy any amount of it.

They made their way into Tamimi's supermarket, bought what they needed and were quickly out, sharing their carrier bags. Mollie suggested they go for coffee at the big café in the square of the Souk. It had a large family corner sectioned off from where the men sat so there was usually space. On arrival they made their way through to the back of the restaurant where a large screen was situated and they looked around. They found most of the tables occupied but there was a family sitting by a wall. A young western-dressed man was there with his wife in niqab and a child was with them. The authorities seemed not to mind single women joining forces with such a group and the sisters asked if they could sit with them.

The young man smiled warmly. 'By all means, ladies.' The young woman moved the little girl so that she sat on her lap and two chairs were released for the sisters. A waiter was passing close by and they ordered coffee with nothing to eat.

Mollie was always more gregarious than Julia and she instigated conversation straightaway. 'We always enjoy the coffee here,' she said.

The young man proved as vocal. 'Same with us. We always choose it when we come in.'

'Do you live near here?' asked Mollie.

'We're in Ratton, so not far.' Mollie was struck by the warmest of smiles on the young man's face. He could not have been more than twenty-two.

'My name's Tony Henderson,' he said. 'This is my wife Judy and our little girl, Fatima.'

The sisters were immediately intrigued by the middle-eastern name but did not allude to it.

'We're sisters. Our name is Chadwick.' Mollie wanted to be friendly but not so that she would disclose their first names, not straightaway. In that she was influenced by Julia's wishes. They both noticed that Judy nodded a lot but said nothing, except when leaning down to speak to their daughter. In due time the coffee arrived and the sisters began drinking.

'It's pointless to ask whether you have always lived in Eastbourne, with everybody having to stay put where they are,' observed Mollie.

'Yes, that's true. My parents were already living here when I came along.' Tony had an infectious laugh. Both sisters thought what a nice chap he was. They kept up a general conversation with him, noting all the time that the wife was not contributing anything to it, no matter what efforts Mollie made to bring her into the pleasant atmosphere that was building. Mollie felt able to ask Tony what his work was.

'I'm with the Regulation Ministry,' he answered brightly.

Mollie winced inwardly but carried on. 'What do you do there?'

'I deal with identification and permissions.'

'So you're one of those responsible for our iqamas?'

'That's a large part of it, certainly, but increasingly I'm concerned with permissions to leave the area.'

'We've often wondered about that.' Mollie attempted to include Julia in the conversation. 'How exactly do you decide who can leave and who can't?'

'Most of it relies on instinct. As you probably know, if someone wants to travel beyond Brighton to the west or Hastings to the east, they have to have a pretty good reason for doing so.' The young man's face smiled even more broadly. 'Anyone requesting going to Southampton for instance doesn't stand a chance.'

'Why is that?'

'He might be trying to get away. We couldn't have that.'

The sisters exchanged a surreptitious glance. Get away to what? More of the same overseas? Attempting to keep things on an even keel, Mollie asked Tony if he enjoyed the work.

'I have to admit most of it is boring. But I only work three days a week: Al-Sabt, Al-Ahad and Al-Ithnayn. The rest of the week is mine so that's all right. The salary is more than enough to keep us going. It gives us plenty of time for our Islamic studies.'

Mollie could not help observing that his wife dropped her head even lower. 'So you are Muslims?'

Tony's face brightened still further and even suggested a note of surprise at the question. 'Oh yes.'

'That would explain your little girl's name.'

'Exactly,' he confided warmly. 'I decided when we got married, we would become Muslim. I did not like the idea of our being perpetually non-Muslim, the only alternative. It's much better than Christianity, which of course is no option anyway. But I was always taken with the idea of there being no God but God. Much more logical to accept Mohammad, peace be upon him, as a prophet rather than a so-called son of God.'

Despite the sisters' bemusement, Mollie chanced her arm.

'Do you have any recollection of life before the Occupation?'

Tony laughed. 'Not in the least, I'm glad to say, not from what my father tells me. No sense of order. Everyone having a computer of their own, being able to say what they liked by sending each other e-mails. We have computers in the office of course, every ministry does. You have to have channels of communication to keep government moving. But it would be incredibly hazardous to have ordinary people possessing them and sending dangerous material everywhere they wanted to. Dad also told me about something called social media. I could hardly believe it; people broadcasting on these various forms, saying what they liked to each other. Awful. I've even heard that women were allowed to drive.' He burst out laughing. 'There's been some talk that in New Arabia, they might allow it. Ridiculous. Couldn't possibly happen. Might have done of course in the old days under the House of Saud.'

Julia thought better of informing him that she had once been a car owner and driver. Now was a time when it was better to leave some things unsaid. Tony Henderson was yet more forthcoming.

'So yes, we are both steeped in Islam now. Little Fatima here will grow up with no untoward influences, Allah be praised. She'll be in a world of good order. I have been thinking that Judy and I will change our names to complete our Muslim identities, but I haven't decided yet.'

The sisters looked at Judy, who continued to say not a word. Tony carried on in his warm and friendly style. 'Where do you ladies live?'

Julia decided it was time she spoke, much to Mollie's relief. 'We're in lower Meads, close to the seafr..., the corniche.'

'Oh very good. I have often thought it would be satisfying to live near the correctional areas.'

Both sisters blinked. Tony Henderson noticed nothing through their veils but carried on.

'That's another massive advantage of being Muslim. Everybody keeps in good order if they know what's good for them.' The smile broadened again. 'I believe a beheading took place this very morning.'

'That's right.' Julia's voice adopted a frozen sound which again Tony missed.

'And of course the old Crumbles area is well-established for adulterous women. Stoning is the only answer to that. Otherwise married life goes to pot.'

Mollie noticed Julia's hands starting to tremble. But she was determined to pursue the matter. She tried to keep as calm as she could.

'I'm intrigued about that. I've been reading that a new law might be brought in so that stoning only applies to women. If that happens, there would be no punishment for men risking their marriages going to pot, as you put it.'

'Yes, the thinking is that we were influenced too much by the old western idea of equality between men and women. But that's preposterous. For example, men can have up to four wives. Naturally though, women can't have four husbands.'

For Mollie, this was the crunch aspect of the Occupation: the divide between the generations. The youngsters had known nothing different and were becoming not just conditioned; they actually preferred the way of life that had taken hold over nearly twenty years. In those circumstances, how could the old life possibly be restored?

'It's one of the changes that are bound to come in,' the young man continued. 'Societies evolve and different things happen from time to time. After all, we are in the year 1439.'

Mollie Chadwick wanted to scream out: 'My God, aren't we just? Aren't we *just*?' Instead she smiled and nodded her head, before turning to her sister. 'Drink up, Julia. We should be going.'

They got up and so did Tony Henderson. He even bowed his head slightly as he said: 'Nice to meet you, ladies. No need to wish you a safe journey home, *inshalla*. Everywhere is safe.'

The ladies made their farewells, still without a word from Judy Henderson who kept her head down, but they did receive a smile from Fatima.

Chapter 5

Friday 10 August 2018

Julia could hardly wait to show him when he arrived for Scrabble that day. 'Just look, Henry.' She was brandishing a copy of *The Week*, opened at the correspondence page. 'It's just arrived. You saw Mollie's letter in last Sunday's *Telegraph*?'

'Oh yes. I thought it was excellent.'

'Well *The Week* has selected it for their pick of the letters page.'

'Well done, Mollie.' Henry immediately felt as elated. Mollie looked on, smiling in some embarrassment. He sat down at his usual place at the table to take a closer look at it.

'This has brought your knowledge about films to bear, Mollie. All those examples you listed.'

'I couldn't stand by and see that reviewer get away with it. Suggesting that up to 1963 there were no films about, let's say, dodgy subjects, and that *The Servant* changed all that.'

'You must have mentioned about a dozen here made before '63. Good for you.'

They got down to their Friday afternoon business but returned to the subject once or twice.

'I particularly liked your comment about Malcolm Muggeridge saying that one of the benefits of older age is that when young historians get things wrong about the past, they can be pulled up by those who were around at the time.'

'Well I certainly felt it when that bloke wrote that up to then we hadn't had anything on the big screen, what did he say again?' Mollie glanced at her letter, 'exploring social taboos. That's why I was so pleased with the *Sunday Telegraph* including a picture from *A Taste of Honey*. If that didn't explore a few social taboos, I don't know what did. I had a fun time working on that one, but in the end the crowd scenes in question weren't used.'

Fortune continued to be with Mollie. In the first game she spotted DRIER on the board and smartly added TAW in front of it coinciding with a useful triple score. Not content with that she cleared her rack in one go with ANODISE. By nearly teatime she was on a high and ready for a rant about the week's events.

'What about all this business in schools and universities these days?' said Mollie. 'Did you hear about the place somewhere in Bucks deciding not to blow a whistle at the end of playtime?'

'No, I missed that,' answered Henry. 'What's that all about?'

'Some nitwit of a head teacher decided that the whistle was too aggressive, and some children could be startled.'

'Oh get away,' said Henry. 'What are they doing then as an alternative to get the kids' attention?'

'The teacher on duty has to raise her hand in the air and – can you imagine this? – wait for pupils to notice the signal.'

Henry roared with laughter. 'Judging by my school days in Hackney, they'd be waiting a dammed long time. Even longer in the playground when I was teaching in Newham.'

'Precisely,' said Mollie.

Julia expressed her own exasperation and left to make the tea.

'Worse than that, what about the school in our own county, banning skirts?'

'Yes, I did see that,' observed Henry. 'I think I could cope with that compared with the, what is it? about a hundred and twenty state schools now letting boys wear skirts to make allowance for those "confused about their gender", so the saying goes. But how many does that refer to?'

'And is it such a reality?' said Mollie. 'We live in such an atmosphere of following one fad after another. Of course the youngsters are going to be impressed by that. I don't know.'

'The parents are up in arms over the trousers thing,' said Henry. 'They're pointing out that their daughters like wearing skirts, so why should they be forced into trousers?'

'It is that question of choice again. Which brings us to the uproar of the week.'

'Oh, old Boris, do you mean?' laughed Henry.

'Exactly,' said Mollie. 'I can't believe the fracas about his article, which was essentially about the right of women to wear the burka and niqab. After the row broke out, I read the article again to see if I had got it wrong. But he was absolutely in favour of their having the choice to wear what they want to. Just the same as those parents at the school who want to see their daughters having the right to wear skirts.'

'Yes, it's the double standards that come into play every time, isn't it? But what did for him was the bit about what he said they looked like when they did wear this gear.'

'I do find this tiresome. They're not satisfied with an argument almost passionately in favour of women having the right to wear what they like. But to think that a harmless joke can let rip an uproar about dog-whistle Islamophobia is just too damned ridiculous. For God's sake, where is the sense of proportion with some of these people?'

'The curious thing,' said Henry, 'is that the comment itself had my attention for a completely different reason.'

Julia caught the tail end as she marched the trolley into the room. 'What comment was that, Henry?'

'The comparison Boris made with letter boxes.'

'Yes, that did cause a stir, didn't it? If it had been a swipe about our own people, there wouldn't have been the slightest comment. But because it involved an ethnic community..... I don't know?'

'But the thing is,' said Henry. 'Their long gowns and head gear are all black.'

'Sorry, not with you,' said Mollie.

'Well, given the colour, how could the women look like letter boxes. Letter boxes are red.'

Mollie and Julia looked blankly at Henry.

'They're red,' he emphasised.

'Oh, you're talking about ours. That's just coincidence. The decorator painted over the slit when he did our door. Never did understand that.'

'No, no,' protested Henry. 'I wasn't talking about ours. I mean the red letter boxes where you post your letters at the corner of the road.'

More blank looks from the sisters. 'But they're not letter boxes, Henry,' protested Julia. 'They're post or pillar boxes.'

'Aren't they letter boxes as well? That's what I've always called them.'

The sisters burst out laughing. 'Then you're an idiot,' ventured Mollie.

Henry laughed as well. 'You don't mean I've had it wrong all these years!'

'Yes, of course you've had it wrong,' said Mollie.

'Ah well, you learn something every day,' said Henry. 'Even so, if Boris meant the personal letter boxes on our doors, well they're not black either.'

'I shouldn't worry about it, Henry,' observed Julia. 'Although I must say Boris wouldn't be too pleased to realise the point he was making has been swept entirely aside in this building. Now then. Who's for tea?'

Chapter 5a

Al-Jum'ah 28 Dhul Qadah 1439

It was a slog for Henry, but he was determined to get there. He had not done the walk for a long time and on this bright morning, he had decided it was time to make the effort. With his weight a problem, he knew he would have to take things slowly. He reached the deserted Holywell kiosk at the foot of the South Downs and gave it a good look as he passed by on the left. Long gone were the days before the Occupation when he enjoyed a walk up to it for a coffee. Now it had a beaten appearance, locked up and forlorn. Henry trudged on past Pinnacle Point and on to the wooded pathway leading to the open coastal downland.

Within minutes he was there, looking down on what had been the playing field for Eastbourne College. Also now deserted, strange to say the wilderness that had taken over the once freshly mown turf had assumed a grandeur of its own. His eyes scanned the total panorama and he sat down briefly on a park bench, glad that the powers-that-be had not managed to alter the natural environment. They could not keep the birds away. Nor had Occupation got rid of the sounds of the crickets in the thick grass. The rabbits too were still darting around in and out of their burrows in the grassland. He closed his eyes and forgot. He managed to forget a lot lately. Increasing age was an increasing help in that regard. The sound of a noisy seagull overhead woke him with a start. The warm summer sun bore down on him and he was ready for the next stretch.

He felt lucky. Living on the coast in Occupation was a great benefit. How must it be for those stuck in the capital in small flats? The constant call to prayer in every part of London must seem never-ending. Here he could escape. So far no authority had forbidden anyone to walk this far out of the town centre. Give it time though. Rumours were abounding that even Beachy Head might be out of bounds soon. The number of suicide attempts had increased slightly despite the patrols up there. It seemed odd to think that The Leader was determined to save life when it was otherwise so disregarded. Perhaps that was it. The Leader wanted to be in control of death as well as life. Made sense, Henry supposed, from a dictator's point of view.

He was finding the going even tougher now. The incline looked gradual. To him it was anything but. He slowed his pace as he continued along and up the ridge that bore slightly inland before emerging again to the top of the ever-rising cliff. The sun and the beauty of the day caught him again and he lost concentration on the politics of life, if you could call it that, where everything was decided and nobody had a say in the scheme of things.

He arrived at the cliff top overlooking Falling Sands which in turn represented the foot of the steep climb up to Peace Path leading directly to Beachy Head. Peace

Path! That seemed a contradiction in terms now. But he forgot all of that as he fell on to the bench seat by the bush with the sea in front of him.

Surveying the glorious sight, he looked everywhere around him, at as much of the three hundred and sixty degrees as he could manage. He noticed a figure way in the distance from whence he had come but whoever it might be was far enough away not to be discernible. He always looked all the way around to see if anyone was within earshot before his next move and his eyes swept the view now before he declared aloud: 'Thank you, God, for all of this.'

Henry always wondered why he said it. He was sceptical about faith although not an atheist. He told himself each time that as he sat on that bench and looked at the sea in front of him and the sweep of the Downs behind, he wanted, even needed, to thank something or somebody for it. The matter always confused him and in these recent years even more so given that his oppressors had the same God but called him Allah. Yet once he had expressed his thanks, he felt relaxed enough to go on with his next set of thoughts. Which were not difficult to decide upon. As he looked in the direction he had come from, the speck of the figure already noted grew larger. Henry could now make out a man much fitter than himself for his walking rate was a lot quicker than his own. Then his mouth tightened. The man was dressed in a white thobe and ghutrah.

He was heading in Henry's direction but would probably turn right at Henry's bench to climb up to the inland path that would take him back on his return trip. The man would pass by him. What was Henry to do? He always took the view that the merest nod towards any stranger clearly of Middle Eastern origin was a form of collaboration. Yet his upbringing kept coming back at him and he could not be intentionally impolite. The man drew ever nearer. To Henry's dismay, he made straight for his bench seat.

'May I join you?' His smile was warm.

'Well, of course,' replied Henry. 'It's free for everybody.' He chuckled awkwardly as he realised the obviousness of his statement.

The man was younger than himself and – Henry could not help noticing – was certainly not overweight. He took a few deep breaths.

'This is my favourite walk.'

'Yes, it is beautiful up here. I don't get up here as much as I used to.'

'Are you originally from Eastbourne?'

'No, but I came to live here over thirty years ago. And you?'

'I was sent over with my family from Iraq at the time of the Occupation.'

Henry's lips tightened. 'You speak very good English.'

The man smiled. 'When you've lived in a place a long time, a lot rubs off.'

Henry felt surprised by the use of such a phrasal verb. He was intrigued and looked carefully in the man's direction. 'You remind me of someone.'

The man smiled. 'My brother is a doctor.'

'Dr al-Katatni?' queried Henry. 'Shefik?'

'That's the man.'

'That's it, I can see the likeness. He's my doctor, and an excellent one.'

'Glad to hear it. He's my older brother.' The man thrust his hand forward. 'Muktar Ali,' he offered.

Henry still felt wary and uncertain of himself but responded anyway, receiving the man's hand. 'Henry Wagstaff,' he mumbled.

There was an immediate silence following the pleasantries, but Henry's curiosity was stirred. It had been known how people were imported from Iraq and elsewhere to Europe to 'train' the natives. He decided to chance his arm. 'You were sent here as a fifth columnist?' His eyes were fixed steadily on the man.

'Oh yes,' he laughed. 'We were sent over to keep the infidels in check. It didn't quite work out that way.'

'How so?'

'Many of us had no such interest. We were forced from our land by our own people and had no incentive to hold up their commands in someone else's. They were not to realise they were doing us a favour.'

'How's that?' asked Henry.

'We had no idea where in this country they would send us. But I did put in a plea to come to this area where my brother was already working. He always spoke so well of this part of the south coast. They agreed to it. I love it here. I'd never want to go back.'

Henry's interest in the man was now tipping over with enthusiasm but he was inclined not to show it too much, determined as he was not to get involved with the opposition.

'How do you feel about being part of the Occupation?'

Muktar Ali turned to face him directly. He spoke quietly and without anger. 'When you have seen your own pregnant sister nearly at the point of birth have her legs forced together so that she and her baby die in agony, you don't have too many concerns as to your effect on others or where you are pushed around.'

Henry Wagstaff was not by nature an emotional person. He had heard enough about brutal punishments while in Saudi Arabia, including those meted out by Iraqis during the brief occupation of Kuwait. But he felt his eyes welling up and he stayed silent until he had regained his composure. In the complete quiet now shared between them, a seagull squawked loudly as it left the bush beside them and flew off above their heads before gliding out to the blue sea. After what seemed an age, Henry cleared his throat.

'You know when I was in Saudi, er, New Arabia, I had the opportunity to learn something about the Arabic past. You have such a history of innovation in science. What a golden age, from the eighth to the fourteenth centuries, as I understand it. Sparked off advances in mathematics, medicine, chemistry, astronomy. Some even say it paved the way for the Renaissance and Enlightenment in Europe. How could such barbarism exist with such a cultural background like that?'

Muktar Ali produced an ironic chuckle. 'You could say the same about a much closer time, in Germany. With all that culture: music, literature, ballet and so on; how could the Nazi mind have commanded such a grip?'

'Point taken.'

'And if it comes to that, consider what you have achieved here. In which light, how come some of your own countrymen can be found baying for blood at the stonings of adulterous women along at the Crumbles?'

Henry stiffened. He knew it was true. It was the same on the occasions when an execution took place at Chopping Square. He realised it was a rhetorical question he was asking. 'Is it really the case, about civilisation being only skin deep?'

Instead of replying, Muktar Ali asked: 'Where were you in Saudi?'

Despite the man's use of the old name of the former kingdom, Henry was wary and determined to be as vague as possible. 'I had two spells out there. One at Yanbu al-Sinaiyah and one at Dhahran.' He wanted particularly to keep the second low-key. 'I much preferred being on the Red Sea coast. The climate was easier and I enjoyed swimming there, diving down and seeing the tropical fish. It was like something out of Jacques Cousteau.'

Muktar Ali shook his head slowly.

'A French sea explorer. He made documentary films.'

The man nodded in understanding.

'It's al-Jum'ah,' observed Henry, changing the subject. 'And you are not at the mosque.'

The man laughed. 'Let's call it Friday, shall we? After all we are in England.'

Henry's face broke into a smile and effortlessly he found himself warming to the man, who continued to go on to surprise him.

'I'm a secular Muslim.'

Henry's eyes opened widely. 'I never knew there was such a thing, I mean a person.'

'Most people do not know it. There are plenty of us though who don't attend the mosque.' Henry's look showed he wanted more explanation. Muktar Ali was content to provide it.

'Are you religious?' he asked.

Henry shrugged and said he did not have a faith especially. He did not attend church.

'There you are then. Notwithstanding that, I expect you see yourself as a Christian by cultural association.'

Henry answered earnestly. 'Oh, certainly.' Ever since the Occupation he was determined to think that way.

'And I am a Muslim by the same criterion. I have no intention though of falling down on my knees half a dozen times a day.'

'You're dressed in a thobe,' observed Henry.

'My type is tolerated,' said Muktar Ali, 'as long as we wear the full rig on….Fridays.' He laughed again. Henry joined him but was still intrigued.

'How do you cope and survive? You have suffered atrocities, been driven out of your homeland to serve a purpose here in a strange land.'

Muktar Ali was confident in his reply. 'You just used the word yourself. It's about survival.'

'At any cost?'

'Almost. I think how lucky I am to have been landed here. I could have been sent to a big city. I might yet. But while I've got this…..' His voice trailed off as he gazed out to sea. The two men shared another silence before Muktar Ali spoke again.

'Do you know a book called *Lavengro* by George Borrow?' Henry shook his head. 'It was written in 1851. There's a dialogue in it between two people. One says that life is sweet. The other asks him if he really thinks it is. The first one replies. "Think so? There's night and day, brother. Both sweet things; sun, moon and stars, brother. Who would wish to die? There's the wind on the heath, brother. If I could only feel that, I would gladly live forever".'

Henry spoke quietly. 'You've remembered that well.'

'I came across the book years ago. A friend gave it to me. Those words impressed me so much that I wanted to remember them always. I've turned up the passage many times.'

Henry stayed quiet, willing him to go on, to cement and confirm his philosophy. It was giving him an inner peace.

The man on the bench turned to face him.

'Experience comes your way. You deal with it. You set your thinking on another plane. Not necessarily a higher one. But a different one. Then you survive. If you don't survive......' He shrugged. 'If I don't survive, I miss all this.' He swept his left arm outwards, as though embracing all that lay before and around him.

Henry did not say anything, but he nodded.

After another silence between them, Muktar Ali changed the mood. 'The Leader will be coming here soon.'

The disclosure had a jolting effect on Henry who looked blankly at him. 'Here?'

'I have one or two contacts who've sent word. He's coming from his base in Geneva to do a tour of the country.'

Henry laughed ironically. 'Like a royal tour of the old days?'

'Something like that. The south coast is included.'

'But surely he won't bother with Eastbourne.'

Muktar Ali appeared certain of his facts. 'The Ramada Hotel is closed off for an entire week next month.'

Henry pursed his lips. 'We haven't had something like that for ten years or more. I suppose we shall all have to attend.'

'I fear so, showing our combined enthusiasm.'

Henry wanted to say so much more to this man, to tell him of his own experience in the Middle East. Sadly he concluded that it would be better to keep his counsel. As discreetly as he could, he checked his watch. 'You will understand if we don't exchange contact details?'

'Of course.'

'I shall look out for you on this patch. It would be good to see you again.'

'Me too.'

Henry stood up. 'Now I must be off for one of those truly important things in life we seemed to be alluding to just now.'

Muktar Ali smiled and looked questioningly up at Henry.

'I'm playing Scrabble this afternoon.'

Chapter 6

✿
♈

Friday 31 August 2018

Henry Wagstaff was in a decluttering mood. He had spent the week so far on clearing out files in his computer. Documents, e-mails, trash, spam had all been subject to a blitz. Now he could not put off what he was least looking forward to: the hard stuff in the cupboards and filing cabinet. At the age of seventy-eight, he was more aware than ever that time was going only one way. There was no family left except for a distant cousin in Australia. His closest friends, Derek and Joan in Lancaster Gate, were not much younger than him. He therefore wanted to get rid of as much as possible before strangers were forced to clear out a lifetime's accumulation of material. He was not sure what to do about his journals. He looked in his glass book cabinet again at the volumes going back more than fifty years, and already covering two shelves with a third about to be encroached upon. There must be plenty of social history there, if only relating to prices of goods! But where to leave them? He must look into that question seriously one day. For now Henry was going to put it off yet again, formulating the excuse that he intended to make a start on the plentiful other material he had built up.

His inspiration was a book he had come across in the Oxfam shop when browsing for more reading material. The title *Living Simply* had caught his eye. Glancing through it, he quickly saw the religious interpretation from its author, Fiona Castle, but he was not keen on the theology it had to offer. The more secular message about decluttering certainly had made an impression and he bought the book. Now he felt almost duty-bound to act on it. But what to start on first?

He peered at the top shelf of the built-in wardrobe that was not used for any clothes. Just as well for it was stacked with box files and folders. It was the line of folders that he was looking at. The first two or three inspired no particular interest so he would leave them for another time – another procrastinating action that Henry recognised but ignored. Then he came upon a thick file labelled 'Saudi Arabia'. He had not looked at it in nearly thirty years and could not hold off any longer the possibility of slimming it down. In any case it caught his interest. He heaved it out of its housing and took it to the desk in his study. It would contain all the material connected with his sudden departure from the kingdom. Henry felt it to be a shining example of material that could be jettisoned without too much ceremony. He opened it up. It was not long before his eyes settled on the newspaper article that had caused the trouble.

The *Eastbourne Herald*, 18 August 1990. The memory flooded back of his being chuffed that they had printed the whole lot: the entire swathe of diary extracts he had sent them. The expectation had been that they might take out a few pieces from it and make up a story. His only regret was that it was all raw diary entry material and the register was not right for a newspaper audience. But the one thing that had not occurred to him in his naivety was to worry about the content itself. Suddenly Henry was back in those stressful times.

Tuesday 14 August 1990. Henry Wagstaff was among one hundred civilian teachers taken by buses to an aircraft hangar behind the administration block of Aeronautics UK on the airbase at Dhahran. They filed in and Henry realised all too clearly that the letters NBC did not in this case refer to an American broadcasting station. Instead they stood for nuclear, biological and chemical. They were given their NBC outfits, designed to protect them from any of the three choice dangers for which they stood. They all sat in semi-circular groups waiting to receive instruction. Henry was with his three friends with whom he had teamed up for whatever social life had emerged. They nattered for a while, their concentration absorbed in what was to come.

An instructor arrived and told them first to put on the trousers and jacket over their day clothes. Henry noticed they were covered with carbon on the inside which naturally came off on the company clothing. The instructor explained about the respirator, which used to be called a gas mask, and showed them all how to put it on. After that the head piece attached to the jacket was to be fitted around the respirator and over the head. It was not long before Henry felt hot and looked around at everybody. It was like something out of *Quatermass II*. He was relieved when they were advised to take off the head covering and the respirator. Then they were introduced to the injection equipment. If an attack happened and there had not been time to don the suits, and in the event of breathing difficulties, Henry needed to inject himself with the substance into the thigh. Let fifteen minutes go by and inject again if necessary. But don't do it a third time. Dick Kenyon sitting next to Henry asked why. The instructor said: 'Because it will kill you. Now then moving on....' It was with such matter-of-factness that the next hour passed in practising putting on the NBC suits in order to increase the degree of swiftness required for the purpose. At the end of the hour's training, Henry and his friends made their way out carrying their suits and kit. They clambered on to their bus to take them back, none of them saying a word on the short journey.

By the time they arrived back at the Corniche Compound, they felt the need to stay together and did not go back to their rooms but remained in the lobby area, flopping out on the comfortable plush furniture. They dumped their NBC suits and kit on the floor and Henry offered to collect four mugs of tea. The others readily agreed. On his way to the machine, Henry was formulating a plan. His misgivings about what was happening were growing. He felt it was futile bringing any of his concerns to the management, locked as they were into a diehard regime, most of them with long-standing careers in the RAF. They clearly thought what they were doing now was a civilian extension of it. In any case they were hidebound by Saudi masters ready to bear down on them at any time. What other reason did the company have for being in the kingdom anyway? Henry arranged four mugs of tea on a tray and carried it to the others.

'Cheers, Harry,' said Dick Kenyon. The others followed suit.

'Where do we go from here, do you reckon?' asked the youngest of the four, Terry Casey.

'Christ knows,' said the oldest, George O'Riordan. He had worked most of his life overseas in technical training and thought he had seen most of what expat life had to offer. This was something new.

'We're told we are free to go any time. But what kind of a Hobson's choice is that? We shall stand to be in breach of contract and have no chance of being employed by them again. We'll lose all our build-up of gains, bonuses and the like. I dunno.'

George was adding ammunition to Henry's plan and there would be more to follow. But he was determined not to say anything about it yet. They went over the events of the previous days that had moved so fast. It was less than a fortnight since Saddam Hussein's troops had invaded Kuwait at two o'clock in the morning. By 6 August drivers were being held up on the local highways as tanks thundered past them on the way north. The following day warships from all over the world were flocking to the Gulf intending a blocking move, including those from the Soviet Union. The day after that George Bush Snr began sending 4,000 paratroopers to Dhahran.

'I see the Brit soldiers have started arriving at this compound today,' observed Henry. He picked up his NBC suit lying next to him. 'I felt incredibly hot in this thing an hour ago, and that was inside in air conditioning. If it comes to war, what's it going to be like for the blokes out in the desert having to wear them?'

'I have heard that if war was to break out right now in this heat,' observed George, 'survival time in these suits would be thirty minutes.'

'My scariest moment was on Thursday,' said young Terry, whose awareness of his wife and two year-old daughter at home in Hull had become acute. 'It was after Bush's broadcast. Commentators on't World Service talked about a possible armoured attack while American forces were getting organised.'

'The old hands here were telling me that if Saddam didn't strike here by four in the morning, he would have lost his chance,' observed George O'Riordan.

Henry had been told the same and he smiled wryly as he was reminded of what he had written in his diary the following day. 'This morning I woke up well after 4am. I was still alive.'

'From my classroom window I have a clear view of the runway,' observed Dick Kenyon. 'Every time I looked out this morning, another U.S. transporter was touching down, disgorging personnel and equipment and taking off again to head north. And each time I turned back to my class to carry on imparting the vagaries of the present perfect tense because we're considered essential staff. All around us U.S. and British forces are obviously gearing up for a war situation. It's Pythonesque.'

The others murmured assent and Henry took careful mental note for the letter he was formulating to the British Foreign Secretary.

'It's pretty obvious, isn't it?' said George. 'If there's any question that we might be subject to a chemical warfare attack, and obviously there is from this afternoon's training session, we should have been out of this place long since.'

Terry thought hard again about his two year-old daughter.

'There's something crazy going on,' continued George. 'The Arabs are not all on the same page anyway. You'd think that Iran who'd fought Iraq for eight years would be onside. But they've said it would take Saddam's side if war breaks out. As it is, Saddam has called on all Saudis to rise up against King Fahd.'

'And did you hear Eric Heffer in the House of Commons lending a cynical note? Dead appropriate though. He reckoned that if Kuwait was steeped in carrots instead of oil, neither us or the Yanks would be in there.'

'Too right, Dick' echoed Terry.

'Except though,' put in George O'Riordan, 'if it had been carrots, Saddam wouldn't be bothering with the place either.'

The group went quiet for a while and they concentrated on their mugs of tea. George broke the silence. 'Come on now, let's cheer ourselves up. Some wag in the staff room this morning suggested a title for a new film. Based on a 60s epic, he came up with *55 Days in Dhahran*.'

Henry noticed that the other two were not being caught by the suggestion so he stepped in to try and help lighten the mood. 'Excellent idea,' he said. 'Have they come up with a cast list yet?'

'I don't think so, Harry,' laughed George.

'Well, let's give it a try,' said Henry. 'Who would you have playing Saddam?'

'Let's see.' George thought for a moment. 'How about one of two: Arthur Mullard or Eli Wallach?'

'Difficult choice, that,' said Dick, warming to the exercise. 'Both similar.'

Even Terry raised a smile. 'What about Mrs Hussein?'

'Surely that would be a shoo-in for Zsa Zsa Gabor.'

More laughter had the group getting into the swing of it and they found themselves taking the matter semi-seriously. 'For George Bush you could have Ronald Reagan or Henry Fonda,' offered Dick.

They decided that either Sid James or George Cole would serve as Sharpie the Flightline Card but it was when George offered up Gloria Swanson or Dame Edna for Mrs Thatcher, that the laughter compounded. It reached a peak on the suggestion of giving the part of Yasser Arafat to Alfie Bass or Bella Emberg.

Henry felt the need to point out that some of the suggested cast were in fact dead.

'Ah well, that's what happens in fantasy, doesn't it?' said George.

At which point the dining room doors opened and the group, still laughing, turned their minds to the evening meal. Picking up their NBC suits and kit, they took them into the dining room to place them by their table. Henry was to observe not for the last time that even in an atmosphere of acute tension and uncertainty, comedy and humour were never far away. It was to continue.

As they entered the room, someone came by and asked if they'd heard the latest about Lord Tennyson. They all shook their heads. Lord Tennyson was the nickname given to a colleague in recognition of his eloquence and powers of expression. He was a great thickset growler working on the Flightline. As one of the 'heavies', the patronising epithet might have been made for him. In a generally homophobic atmosphere, Lord Tennyson had taken it on himself to safeguard what he saw as the moral well-being of the men. People had grown accustomed to passing his door with a notice thereon. It declared the sage advice: 'Don't Bend for a Friend'. It was accompanied by a graphic diagram in case Lord Tennyson's readers had not got the point.

'You wouldn't believe,' said the chap at the dining room door talking to Henry's group. 'Some wag has come along this afternoon and written underneath in felt-tip: "Why, is it alright with a stranger?" He'll be livid when he sees it.' The group burst out laughing. They went into the dining room and found themselves a free table for a foursome. Henry reflected how tiresome he found all the homophobia. Being uninterested either way, he always saw himself looking from the outside at the various quirks and prejudices arising from sex. Particularly aggravating was the inconsistency, not to say hypocrisy involved. There was one character with a black wife at home. Naturally he was infuriated by any racist talk. Yet he was one of the most ardent verbal queer-bashers on the station.

The Sri Lankan waiters began their work, as always with consummate efficiency, to the extent that some of the diners found it irritating to have their plates whipped from under their noses as soon as the last mouthful had been consumed, sometimes even earlier. The foursome looked quickly at the menu and gave their orders.

Suddenly there was uproar at the dining room entrance. Lord Tennyson nearly filled the doorway.

'Oo the fuck has written that fuckin' filth under my fuckin' proper notice?'

The silence lasted a split second before the gathering spotted the irony. The entire dining room was convulsed. Lord Tennyson's face changed to an alarming shade of puce. He turned on his heel and stormed out, kicking over a chair in his path. He never lived it down. The notice was ripped off his door and not seen again.

Twenty-eight years later, Henry sat back on the upright chair in his study and sighed in remembering anew the experience that had brought him in contact with plenty of both the good and the bad of British male expatriate life. He surveyed the material he had just gone through and realised wistfully that so far he had not discarded much of it as he had hoped. A few papers here and there. The main thrust of it though he felt he could not get rid of, well, not just yet. He wanted to keep the records of the bones of the whole episode. Exactly why, he could not work out. It would all go when he died. He looked at the clock.

Henry decided he must leave it now anyway and come back to it tomorrow morning. For now it was time to get the bread pudding organised for the afternoon. Which reminded him. He cursed inwardly that he had forgotten to buy from Sainsbury's some more candied peel which otherwise he always included in the recipe. He wouldn't have enough for the usual two ounces recommended for the bake. He hoped Julia would not notice.

Chapter 6a

✿

Al-Jum'ah 19 Dhul Hijjah 1439

'By the way, Henry, it was Aeronautics UK that you worked for in Saudi Arabia?'

'That's right, Julia.'

'I thought so. I've kept today's *English Arab News* out for you in case you hadn't spotted it. There's a report of someone there in your time who's just died.'

'Really? Who's that?'

'A man called Peter Bartlett.'

Henry chuckled. 'Good lord. That preposterous old goat. A Colonel Blimp if ever I met one. So many of them were, coming straight from the RAF into a civvie company where they felt they could keep one foot in the services. How old was he?'

'Getting on, well, like us, I s'pose,' laughed Julia. She referred to the paper on the table beside her. 'Eighty-seven.'

Henry thought for a moment. 'Yes, that would be about right. Twenty-eight years ago he was just coming up to sixty. Retirement was not too far away when I crossed swords with him.'

Mollie was itching to speak. 'Before you move any more tiles around, Henry, you might credit me with the seven-letter word I've just put down.' Mollie was proud to have captured WEEKEND, having taken advantage of placing the D neatly under the vertically-positioned COLLIDE.

'Sorry, Mollie. Yes, of course. Plus fifty points, that gives you....'

'Ninety-four.' Mollie had already worked it out.

Henry's mind was now in two places. He looked carefully at the remaining D still clear and realised he could make use of it. No seven-letter word to follow hers, but he fitted LOADER on to the board.' Now it was Julia's turn.

Henry turned his attention back to Julia's news and he reached for the paper which in general he had given up reading, although he still took it as it was delivered freely. But the death of Peter Bartlett gave him pause. He was surprised the *English Arab News* had made any mention of it, given that with the revolution and the downfall of the House of Saud, Aeronautics UK had been sent packing without too much ceremony. Mollie realised that he was preoccupied. 'Is that the man who saw to it you were dismissed?'

'No, strangely it wasn't him. I thought it would be after taking the action I took.'

'You mean there was more than one,' laughed Mollie. 'I thought you'd already done enough to get deported, from what you told us.'

'I never went into it fully with anybody,' said Henry. 'It all seemed much simpler to stay with the bare bones of it.'

Julia looked up from her rack. 'You've got us both intrigued now, Henry.'

'Well, it was just that to start with, I decided I was unhappy with the way we were being treated, and I wrote to the Foreign Secretary of the time. Do you remember Douglas Hurd?'

They both nodded.

'What was this, on your own or did you involve others?' asked Mollie.

'That was just the thing. I felt sure I was putting my head on the line and because of that I did not want to include anybody in it. I made that absolutely clear. But at the same time I told a few of my mates out there and sure enough word got around. That's when Colonel Blimp came into it, who's just died.'

'So what happened?' asked Julia.

Henry thought for a moment. 'Do you know it's funny. I haven't got a scrap of records for that time. Before the Occupation, I had a massive folder full of the papers to do with the whole business. They were the first to go in the burn-up as soon as we were taken over. But I do recall that surreal interview with Bartlett.'

He proceeded to tell the sisters about it, holding up their Scrabble session for some time as he unfolded the events of the day in August 1990.

At 10.30 Henry went with his line manager to the office of Peter Bartlett, the Technical Education Manager. They crossed the ground in the intense heat of mid-morning from the School of English to the admin block. Henry was sure the chickens would come home to roost as a result of his letter to the British Foreign Secretary. They were ushered into the man's office and after shaking hands, Bartlett invited them both to sit down. As soon as Henry did, it was as though he knew instinctively the strategy that he was going to adopt. He would attempt to sit in the one fixed position and maintain eye contact with Bartlett all the time. Except for one or two moments during the ninety minutes he was there, he did just that.

Bartlett started off in an affable tone and to Henry's surprise kept it that way for a long time.

'I have asked you over here in the presence of your line manager, Harry, to discuss anything that is troubling you as I am wondering why you decided to write to the Foreign Secretary.'

Henry was annoyed straightaway. In the three years he had been in the place, this man had never addressed him by his first name, much less the diminutive form of it. In fact he could not recollect being called anything at all when on the odd occasion they had met.

Henry adopted his fixed look. 'I decided to write to the Foreign Secretary because I do not have faith in the company, and I wished to raise complaints at a higher level.'

'Oh, you have complaints, have you?'

Determined not to disclose much of the content of the letter until he had heard from the Foreign Office in London, Henry dealt only with the events of Wednesday 8 August and the company's failure to get the staff off the air base between the time of President Bush's announcement of American forces being sent to Dhahran and the time of their arrival in mid-afternoon at the earliest.

Bartlett said that that was a decision that had to be made in Riyadh by the British Ambassador. It was to him that Henry should be addressing his complaints.

For Henry it was the first moment of incredulity in the interview. 'Are you saying, Mr Bartlett, that there is no-one here who can make a decision to evacuate the buildings of this air base in the event of an emergency?'

'Well, I wouldn't say that, Harry. Supposing that in the School of English there was a sudden inflow of noxious fumes. In that case I would expect your line manager, Archie here, to evacuate the building, preferably with the consent of the Saudi Commandant of course. But for anything of a higher level, no, we have to take our instructions from Riyadh.'

At that point the telephone rang. Bartlett picked it up and deployed the courtesy title normally used by others to introduce himself. 'Mr Bartlett here.......Oh, it's all right, sir. I've got the man here now. We're just talking about it. I'll speak to you later, sir.'

He replaced the receiver and, nodding in its direction said to Henry: 'The Base Manager. Now then, Harry. Where were we? Oh yes. You see, the principle I have always lived by is to have complete faith in my superiors.'

Henry's eyes opened wide. 'Have you, Mr Bartlett?'

Bartlett had spotted nothing of the irony in Henry's voice. 'Oh yes, Harry, because if you don't have faith in your superiors, you can't win a war.'

It was later that a catalogue of examples flowed into Henry's mind. In the spontaneity of the moment the only images flashing through his brain were the Charge of the Light Brigade, Gallipoli, and the Somme.

Bartlett moved on to the subject of chemical warfare. Protective suits had been issued so that people could feel reassured with such a measure of protection.

Henry interrupted with: 'And as a public relations exercise back home?'

To Henry's surprise, Bartlett responded enthusiastically. 'Oh yes!' But then: 'There is no question of chemical warfare coming in our direction. Any action that does take place will do so on the border up north.'

Henry felt ready to fire his first salvo. 'In that case, Mr Bartlett, why did one of the instructors at the practice session preface his remarks to a group with the observation: "The chance of a chemical attack on Dhahran is very strong"?'

Bartlett chortled. 'Oh, you don't want to take any notice of that, Harry. You don't know military types. He was probably a chap who had been in the RAF and said that to be sure of gaining the group's attention. I do assure you, you are much safer here than on the concourse at Gatwick.'

Henry did not observe that true or false, he knew precisely where he would prefer to take his chances right then. Instead he brought up the question that had been at the forefront of all the teachers' minds – that of their having the NBC suits and kits while the Saudi cadets they were teaching went empty-handed. The present scenario was that in the event of an attack and having to put the suits on, the next step would be that the teachers would live and the cadets would die.

Bartlett replied: 'Well, of course in time of war we are all faced with moral dilemmas. But in any case the Royal Saudi Air Force are beginning to equip the cadets with protective suits.'

Then it was that Bartlett used the opportunity to say, spreading his arms wide: 'We have said from the start that anyone is free to leave.'

'Yes, Mr Bartlett, but in breach of contract and with no hope of future employment with the company.'

'Oh yes, that is the company's policy.'

'Well, I have no wish to be placed in the position of breaching a contract. Up to now I have been happy to work here. The accommodation is good, so are the support services, and in the three years I have been here, I have been reasonably contented.'

Bartlett's face lit up. 'Indeed. It is an excellent company and the best *I* have ever worked for.'

Henry recalled his having heard that Bartlett had been in the RAF for decades and this was the first and only company he had ever known. But he let it pass. Bartlett then went on to express the confusion in his mind as to why Henry had gone so far to the top rather than talk to someone in management.

'Who did you say you had written to?'

'The Foreign Secretary with a copy to the Secretary of State for Defence.'

'Oh, Tom King?'

'Yes.'

'Oh well, he was here only a couple of months ago. He'll certainly recognise the address when he gets your letter. Anyone else?'

'A copy to the leader of HM Opposition.'

Bartlett looked blankly at Henry. 'Mr Kinnock?'

Henry nodded. Bartlett said: 'What ever for?'

Henry observed that since it concerned a highly important political issue, he had found it natural to act in that way. He had debated in his mind whether to send that particular copy to Gerald Kaufman, the Shadow Spokesman for Foreign Affairs, but he had decided it should go to Neil Kinnock.

Bartlett shook his head and said: 'How curious. Well, I suppose if he thinks he can get a few votes out of it, he'll take whatever action accordingly. Mrs Thatcher of course has taken the right action – as she usually does – in sending British troops out here and Mr Kinnock will go along with her if he thinks he can get a few votes out of it.'

But he still could not understand what Henry had hoped to achieve. 'After all, you will get a brief note from someone in the Foreign Office and they will send the letter through Aeronautics UK's various channels. It will float down to me for comments and I shall send it all the way back again through the same channels. You will certainly have incurred a lot of letter-writing by your action.'

Henry disregarded all the flannel and responded. 'Look, Mr Bartlett, we are into the third week of this crisis. In all that time we have not been addressed once by any member of the management team.'

'But good heavens, Harry. We are all busy people. The Base Manager is working sixteen hours a day, for instance. I hand over notices to all the group leaders, like Archie here, for them to pass on to all their people. There is just not the time to do anything else.'

No, reflected Henry to himself. But you're prepared to spend close on one and a half hours with me on my own now in an attempt to wheedle out of me what I have written to Douglas Hurd.

The meeting was drawing to a close. Henry's line manager Archie reported that one teacher had said to him the previous week that rather than do his usual job, he would much prefer to be out filling sandbags in the fight against Saddam.

'Yes indeed,' echoed Bartlett, on receiving music to his ears. 'In fact I could show you letters, Harry, from people who have said they wish to stay here even if hostilities break out.'

He rose from his chair and expressed the hope that he had been able to put Henry's mind at rest. Henry did not respond. Then Bartlett observed: 'Well, I hope you will think carefully about what I have said.'

To that Henry was able to reply truthfully: 'I shall certainly do that. But I say this, Mr Bartlett. We are a matter of two hundred and fifty miles from Kuwait City. You will know better than anyone how many civilian workers are here, going into the hundreds. If Saddam Hussein had reached here before President Bush's forces last week, you would have had a mass hostage situation on your hands, which would have included you. We would then have been in the position of the eighty-two British men, women and children rounded up from the Regency Palace Hotel in Kuwait City and dispatched to army camps as human shields.'

Bartlett's back stiffened. He came the closest during the entire encounter to losing his affability. 'Well, Saddam Hussein did not reach here, did he?'

Archie Camden took hold of Henry's arm and hurried him out of the office.

Mollie was still turning over her letters in fascination at Henry's story. 'But you didn't get the sack for taking those particular steps?'

'Quite the reverse,' answered Henry. 'They promoted me; gave me my own language laboratory.'

From the other end of Chessington Gardens came the cry over the loudspeaker: *Allahu Akbhar*.

Julia returned to toying with the tiles on her rack. 'So that had nothing to do with the newspaper article you told us about that got you deported?'

'Nothing at all. I'd thought I'd got away with it.'

'It was odd that this man Bartlett was so sure you were safe where you were.'

'Wasn't it?' said Henry in response to Mollie's observation. 'After I was chucked out and Desert Shield broke out into Desert Storm three to four months later, the heaviest loss of life occurred only a mile from the compound where I was staying.'

'Did it?' asked Julia.

'There was a warehouse taken over as a billet for American forces. Saddam sent a Scud missile over and it wasn't intercepted by one the Allies' Patriot missiles. It hit the warehouse and twenty-eight young Americans died. I've sometimes thought of the day I was coming out of a bookshop in Al Khobar. An American serviceman was just walking in and I held the door open for him. He looked me straight in the eye and greeted me. I said: "Hi, how are you doing?" His reply with a smile was "Pretty good". He told me he was staying in the warehouse. I've often wondered about him.'

Chapter 7

❀

Saturday 1 September 2018

Having got the bit between his teeth the previous day, Henry decided to carry on with his decluttering exercise, and particularly with his Saudi Arabia folder.

Then he came upon what he had written on that fateful day, in the shakiest of hands, as he had recorded the meeting a few hours afterwards. After all he had risked, with the letter to the Foreign Secretary and the disclosure of part of it in *The Guardian*, a stupid miscalculation on his part had blown it for him. It was the morning of Monday 24 September 1990. The Base Manager had been called suddenly to Riyadh by the British Ambassador. Henry was summoned to the Deputy Base Manager's office.

He arrived in the admin block. He detected an air of grimness from everyone he spoke to: assistants, secretaries, anyone. Henry was asked to wait in an outer office. The Deputy Base manager, a man called Benton, was with a naval attaché. He could not have been with him long for Henry was soon called in.

It was a large room. At one end of it was a big desk, behind which sat the Deputy Base manager. In front of the desk were two chairs, one of them empty, to which Henry was ushered. In the other was a large figure whom Henry did not know and to whom he was not introduced. Henry noticed that this other man kept his head down from the start.

As soon as Henry sat down, Benton cleared his throat. He was noticeably younger than the other bigwigs in the place and Henry immediately formed the impression that Benton was about to embark on something somewhat out of his league. He thrust a document in front of Henry.

'Do you recognise that?' The voice was a mixture of anger and uncertainty.

Henry saw that it was a photocopy of his article that had appeared in the *Eastbourne Herald* and which they had printed under the headline: 'One week in the shadow of Saddam.' By then it was well over a month old.

Because of the atmosphere and the tone, Henry knew that he was done for. But he determined to be as casual as he could and to play on the young official's uncertainty.

'Oh, yes. That was something I wrote several weeks ago.'

Henry was right. Benton was caught unawares. He took a deep breath. Henry would not have been surprised to see steam coming out of the young man's nostrils.

'Have you any idea how many times you have broken your contract in this article?'

'No, I don't think so.'

'Well, consider this, for instance.' Benton went on to point out a paragraph near the beginning in which Henry had expressed doubt as to King Fahd's credibility in view of his statement that the deaths of fourteen hundred people in a tunnel at the Hadj had been an 'act of God'.

Henry thought there was nothing to lose now, whatever he said. He would therefore go for broke.

'Mr Benton. This was an article in the local newspaper of a seaside town in southern England.' Henry decided on a disingenuous approach, though not entirely. 'It doesn't seem feasible to me that it would get into the hands of Saudis.'

Benton's eyes opened wide. 'Don't you realise the number of Saudis there are in Britain? Any one of them could have seen the article and telephoned the Saudi Embassy.'

'I find it highly unlikely that a Saudi would have run across this in a provincial paper in a coastal corner of south-east England. And even if they had, it's taken them enough time if they're that bothered. The article is already six weeks old.'

By then Benton was fuming. 'I am amazed that you could write such an article in view of your having been spoken to over the other matter.'

'You are talking about my letter to Douglas Hurd.'

'Of course.'

Henry continued to play his cards as best he could. 'I can tell you that the letter to the Foreign Secretary was written well after this article that seems to have caused so much concern.'

Benton's nostrils were still at full flap. 'In that interview with Mr Bartlett, you said you had written to the Foreign Secretary because you did not have any faith in the company. It is a great pity you didn't because you are now summarily dismissed and today is your last day of paid service. You will have to pay for your air fare home and you will leave either tomorrow night or the night after that. If the Saudis knew about this, you would be lucky not to be in jail. This conversation is being recorded. Is there anything you wish to say?'

Henry took a deep breath and attempted a measured response. 'Only to reiterate that any anxieties I might have had existed over the letter to the Foreign Secretary. I'd seen no risk in writing to a local newspaper in Britain as I did. And from what you have just disclosed, despite what you suggested, no Saudi does know about this. I'll therefore say nothing further until I have consulted my solicitor at home.'

Benton bristled. 'Much good that will do you!'

Possibly, thought Henry, but he would give the company something to ponder about, even though he knew his chances were slim. Despite the bravado, it was a fair cop. Although he hadn't said a word against the company in the article, it put them in an embarrassing position with their repressive masters. He knew well enough there was no free speech in a nation like this. He would though have his answers ready the next time he heard anybody at home bleating on about Britain being a police state.

There was no attempt to shake Henry's hand. He arose from the chair as the unspeaking man next to him did the same. It proved to be his task to take Henry through all the procedures involving a departure certificate and to Movements who would arrange a flight home. The unnamed man spoke for the first time as he walked Henry across the courtyard.

'You know apart from the first paragraph, I enjoyed your article.'

Henry was so absorbed in what he had written nearly thirty years earlier that he didn't realise his entry phone buzzer was going. He hurried to the phone to discover that the postman was wanting to deliver a large package. He allowed him entry to leave it on the downstairs hall table. Then he returned to his study and looked at the clock. It would be time to get on with preparing lunch but he could not resist returning to the matter in hand.

Henry sorted through some other papers and came across letters from his solicitor, whose advice he had enlisted on arriving home in September 1990.

He harrumphed again at the thought of being misled about the Saudis having known of the offending article. He had always had his doubts. His solicitor had established that the company had got to learn of the article because it was the family of a local Sussex man also working out there who had got in touch with the company.

Of course that would have been the case. Aeronautics UK would have done everything possible not to let the Saudi authorities know about it. They had got rid of Henry at the first opportunity, naturally so in order to keep their noses clean.

Henry sighed again, and came across a couple of photos of the time, taken when they were wearing their protective suits against chemical and biological warfare. He looked askance at how well-proportioned he was in those days, before piling on the pounds, or even the kilos.

It was a lovely summer weekend. Henry resolved to do something about his weight and would make a start by going swimming in the sea this afternoon, as he did on most Saturdays in the holiday season.

Chapter 7a

Al-Sabt 20 Dhul Hijjah 1439

Henry knew it was the first of September. He had checked it carefully because the day was exceptionally warm. In fact it was so hot that he had made an extra check to see whether the summer was that advanced. He lay on the beach in the glorious late afternoon sun on this Saturday as he insisted on naming the day of the week. Men were allowed to sunbathe and swim on this stretch of the beach at Eastbourne at what used to be referred to as Holywell. All the beach huts had been taken over by the authorities as changing rooms. The whole area was screened off and forbidden to women who enjoyed the benefit of it on days that were once called Mondays and Wednesdays.

Henry lay on his back and heard the waves drifting quietly but firmly against the beach. There were not many people around. Ever since the start of the Occupation, whenever he rested on this beach, his mind travelled back to the beach in the part of the world where his present occupiers came from. And particularly to one night at the same time of year, four weeks after Saddam Hussein's occupation of Kuwait. Henry drifted into that floating world, halfway between consciousness and sleep.

Tonight I have walked across the patch of desert to the seafront, the corniche. It takes only ten minutes from the Corniche Compound. In the darkness I am standing on the Gulf Coast and feeling the peace and quiet, broken only by the whirr of the occasional American helicopter patrolling the coastline. All I can see is the red and green lights blinking away from the choppers.

There is not another sound, or a sight, in the darkness. It is difficult to imagine that over the horizon the Gulf is stiff with warships lined up from all over the world, and somewhere to the left of me, way along the coast, are those innocents carefully guarded as hostages. We think of them constantly.

Yet even more difficult to conjure up in this darkness and peace is that only two hundred and fifty miles along to the left, less than the distance from Eastbourne to Plymouth, Saddam Hussein has tonight proclaimed Kuwait as Iraq's nineteenth province, and renamed Kuwait City to his own liking.

This part of the Gulf Coast at Al Khobar, just outside Dhahran is not much to look at. But it is the sea, and after settling in Eastbourne all those years ago and having become used to the sea, I am glad of it. In the darkness I look to my right and try to imagine the sweep of Eastbourne's western lawns and promenade, slowly rising to the beauty of the South Downs that come to a sudden end as though sliced through by a cheese cutter exposing the white chalk cliffs. Instead I see the lights stretching away along the causeway that connects us with the island of Bahrain. At such times I yearn for the Sussex coastline again.

Meanwhile we are well into the fourth week of the Gulf crisis. For many of us it is the predominating thought last thing at night and first thing when our alarm clocks wake us a few hours later.

It is odd though to feel at the same time a sense of settling down. Everything is in place for a momentous fight, yet there is no sign of one. Already we are beginning to equate the situation with the period of the phoney war between September 1939 and the early summer of 1940. This is the time to be watchful. The last thing we need is to develop a false sense of security.

But the flow of personnel and equipment, especially from the United States, goes on apace. A friend on the flightline recently saw three transporters and two Jumbo jets touching down within the space of half an hour one afternoon.

There are those of us who believe that Saudi Arabia will never be the same again. There are those who believe that would be no bad thing and that the time is long overdue for the medieval aspects of this society to be removed. Restrictions on women are especially severe. Last week I was in a café when a western woman came in. She asked for a cup of tea and the assistant said she would have to drink it outside as there was no 'family corner' provided. Wearily she took her tea and stood outside in the heat to drink it while I stayed inside in the cool. Such a thing could not happen in Bahrain, less than twenty miles away, where women can drive, work as hotel clerks alongside men and do a whole range of jobs denied to them in Saudi Arabia.

Time's getting on. The one or two Saudi fathers playing on the beach with their children in the dark have gone home. So have the American helicopters apparently. All I can hear now is the gentle rippling of the Gulf waves on this hot night. Just a quick look to the left again in the direction of Kuwait – as from tonight the nineteenth province of Iraq. But the coastline is silent and dark.

Henry woke with a start. The sound of the waves had increased during his dreamy state as the tide rose higher on the Eastbourne beach. In the continuing warmth of the day he got to his feet and headed towards the water. He plunged in. Always a strong swimmer, his added weight of recent years propelled him even faster through the salt water. He ploughed a short way in the direction of Beachy Head, returned, and accomplished several lengths along the same stretch. For ten minutes or more he forgot everything about this life. It could have been like the old days when mixed bathing was the norm. The one advantage over former times was that there were always far fewer people around now.

Henry decided that he had achieved enough for one day and so returned to his base. Grudgingly he reflected on another advantage, that of being able to leave belongings including valuables unattended in the knowledge that they would always be safely found. He dried himself thoroughly but as it was still warm, humidly so, he continued to rest on the beach and took out a flask of fruit juice from his haversack to enjoy a cool drink.

His mind had still not completed its reflections, frequently the case when he was here on the beach and mainly alone. One of them centred on the thinking back home after he had lost his job in September 1990. Some people were violently against any action taken against Saddam Hussein for his occupation of Kuwait. They saw a war looming, and they were right. Saddam had resisted all demands by the United Nations to get out of Kuwait and so the short war began in January 1991. Henry could not see any alternative that would have been right.

Ted Heath had managed to get the British hostages out by going over to Baghdad himself to meet one of the world's most obnoxious villains. But how could other acts of war crime be stopped?

Heather Rennison, an English woman married to a Kuwaiti reported starkly enough at the time.

'A cousin of my mother-in-law was arrested. She was only 19. They had found two-way radios in her bedroom. Three days later they came to her home to ask her parents for clothes and blankets. So her parents thought she would be all right. Then the Iraqis hanged her and dumped her body outside her home. There were burns from electricity on her arms and legs. Of course the Iraqis kept the clothes and blankets.'

A bearded man had told the journalist Robert Fisk: 'I had two neighbours who the Iraqis thought were in the resistance. So they pushed them into drains, closed the grille, poured petrol on them and set them on fire. Their families buried them later – you can't leave bodies in drains.'

'What kind of people would burn libraries and museums?' asked Robert Fisk as he wandered through the ravaged streets of Kuwait City after the war had ended in February 1991.

Henry Wagstaff took the deepest sigh as two further reflections overtook him. The worst of it had been on arrival home: the lack of knowledge of people here. It was passing them by, until the night in January when George Bush Snr had sent in the warplanes. Then they sat up.

And so had Henry. Up to this very day on the beach at Eastbourne in his now occupied land, he had nurtured one considerable regret – that he had not been out there with his working colleagues during the month of war. As much as he was relieved to be out of it and back in the safety of Eastbourne, as it was in the old days, he was sorrowful that he could not share what his mates had gone through. He told himself yet again that there was no point in continuing with such regrets, even though he constantly returned to them.

But the insanity of those people in authority in the Middle East and what they were capable of had come sharply into focus the day it became clear that the Occupation would take place here. By then he had long before left the Dental Estimates Board, where he'd taken a job on returning home instead of carrying on teaching, but had retained several links with medical people connected there. Through them he had taken one particular precaution. As twilight descended on the beach at Eastbourne and Henry began getting dressed, he was given another reminder of his action.

The sound of a helicopter began to attract his attention. He looked up to watch its tiny lights coming into view overhead. He might have been back on the beach at Al Khobar, except that instinct told him why this helicopter was appearing from the direction of Beachy Head. In the old days it was a frequent sight, its deployment simply to pick up a body lying at the foot of the cliffs. These days the area was well patrolled. A determined suicide had to use all his or her guile to avoid the military. There was no need for a chaplaincy up there now. No, if there was to be any attempt to do away with oneself, less obvious means were required.

Yet again Henry was motivated to check as he often did the right-hand pocket in his trousers. By habit there was always a clean linen handkerchief in it. He opened it out. It was still there, his insurance policy if the situation became too much. A cyanide pill.

Chapter 8

Friday 7 September 2018

'How did you enjoy the show last night?'

Mollie shuffled her tiles around. 'I loved it, but I always do with any production of *Cats*.'

'I wish I could say the same,' said Julia. 'I really do try, but I can never feel anything personal with the content. People rave about it, but it always leaves me cold.'

Mollie laughed. 'It's the anthropomorphic element, I think, Julia; the idea of people dressing up as animals.'

'Oh, I'm sure you're right. It's always so well done though. Costumes, choreography, everything really about the production, it's always spot on. But I do wonder why they bother.'

'What do you think, Henry? You're surely reviewing it for tonight's programme.'

'In fact, no, Mollie. One of my occasional assistants is as fanatical about it as you are, so I let her have the press tickets. She's recorded her review. And yes, she is raving about it.'

'That's interesting. You didn't want to see it yourself?'

Henry turned his nose up. 'No, I've seen it so many times. I find emotional musicals difficult to take these days. It's like *Les Miserables* and *Blood Brothers*. All that over-emotive passion, oiling its way to a standing ovation at the end. Can't be doing with it. I must be getting old.'

Both sisters laughed. 'I know what you mean,' said Julia.

'I've always been struck though by Eliot's book that the show was taken from.'

'I don't know it.'

'We looked at it when I was at college, Julia,' said Henry. '*Old Possum's Book of Practical Cats*. 'It was a lot of fun, and it made quite a change from the heavy turgid old stuff we had to study on the English course. I was never an academic.'

'There now. How's that for a word?' Mollie laid out the tiles in a contented fashion. She was indeed pleased to have come up with JACKPOT. Henry recorded her score and moved on with his next turn. Mollie got up to collect something from the sofa. Bringing it back to the table she flipped through its pages until settling on a point of interest.

Julia watched her. 'That's something I find tiresome. Theatre programmes. I can remember when they constituted a small booklet of no more than half a dozen pages.'

'Couldn't agree more,' said Henry, his concentration split between what Julia was saying and the open J that Mollie had just created on the board. 'A page outlining the action, another with the cast names, perhaps another noting what would be on next week. Threepence or sixpence would do it. Now look at what you had to buy for the important material last night?' He glanced at what Mollie was holding. 'Packed with information nobody's asked for.' And so saying, Henry opened the dictionary beside him. An idea had just struck.

'Oh, I don't know,' said Mollie. 'I quite enjoy the articles about the author, composer, or whoever it might be. Take this, for instance, one of a number of quotes by T S Eliot that caught my eye.'

Mollie pushed the programme in front of Henry as he was grappling with the pages of the dictionary. He succeeded in not showing that he was put out and followed Mollie's right index finger. In order to hide further his irritation, he read aloud what she was pointing at.

'Liberty is a different kind of pain from prison.'

'Fascinating, don't you think?' asked Mollie.

She had captured Henry's attention for a moment and he took his mind away from the dictionary. He repeated the quotation. 'Not sure I get what he was driving at.'

'I am.'

Both Mollie and Henry looked directly at Julia following her emphatic assertion. They waited for her to go on.

'I feel it at times. Not enough to do. Too much liberty. Not now, not *just* now. These Friday afternoons are different. They're so absorbing. I never have such thoughts then. Or like last night at the theatre. Much as I don't care for *Cats*, I was glad to be there. But so much of the rest of the time….' Her voice started trailing off. 'I think T S Eliot was on to something when he said that.'

Henry's mind was now taken completely off the Scrabble board. 'I do know what you mean, Julia. It happened to me when I was given the push from Saudi Arabia. Couldn't settle. I missed all my mates. I was worried about them. I had a lot of money to see me through a few months and I didn't do anything. I had liberty all right. And it was hard to deal with.'

'I didn't know what to make of it at first,' said Mollie. 'But listening to you both now, it gets clearer. It strikes me that if liberty is to work at all, it has to be accompanied by discipline, or rather self-discipline. It doesn't happen to any of us now, but when we all had to get up early to work for someone else, the discipline was exerted by that someone else. When it's down to us and we have to be our own disciplinarian, that's when problems can arise.'

'Heavens, that's true. How often do you hear people of our age saying they must have something to get up for? I always have something to get up for. It's just that often I don't want to get up *for* it.'

The three of them laughed at Henry's observation. He went on.

'Fortunately, when I do get up, I have plenty to get on with. The radio programme. Still a supporter of Eastbourne Town. Swimming at the pool in the winter, the sea in the summer. Theatre and cinema. Leading guided walks around Meads. That reminds me. Isn't it next Tuesday, Mollie, that I am taking Joyce around Meads?'

'Indeed it is. She was on the phone only last night. She said she is looking forward to it, getting to know about the area that she likes staying in.'

'How long is she here for?'

'Coming Monday and going back Thursday.'

'That's good. And perhaps she'd like to come with us to the Eastbourne Society evening on Tuesday. You've heard about the change of plan.'

'No, what's that, Henry?'

'The speaker has fallen through so they're showing a film that will interest you.'

'Really? Which one?'

'*Death By Prescription.*'

Mollie's eyes opened wide. 'No! That takes me back more than thirty years. Old Bodkin Adams still couldn't fail as box office. We did a lot of filming around here. I can see all those 1950s cars now lined up along St John's Road. It was the first time I really thought it would be nice to live here. I had a lot of fun on that. Most of my scenes finished up on the cutting room floor, par for the course. But I did get a look-in on the sea front scenes, walking up and down in front of the Cavendish.'

'I remember seeing it on television with Timothy West as the doctor. I thought it would have been good enough for the cinema.'

'I quite agree,' said Mollie. 'Well in a sense it will get it now, being shown on the big screen at St Saviour's Hall.'

'I hope you will come along with us, Julia,' said Henry. 'It'll get rid of some more of your liberty time, so that liberty will become a joy rather than a pain?'

Julia smiled. 'Yes, I would like to see the film.'

'Excellent,' exclaimed her sister. 'I have been trying for ages, Henry, to get her to join the Society. Perhaps now she will.'

Henry frowned for a moment. 'Only one thing about next Tuesday that you might be able to help me out with.'

'What's that?' asked Mollie.

'Well, I'm meeting Joyce at 10.30. But it's the day I'm having a water softener installed. They're supposed to be arriving at 9 o'clock and they say it's bound to take a few hours. Could you look after them once I leave?'

'Yes, of course, Henry,' said Julia. 'We'd be glad to.' Mollie echoed her sister's sentiments.

'Thanks,' said Henry. 'That would be a help.' He returned to the word on his mind for the Scrabble game they were still in. Mollie got up to take the theatre programme out of the way to make further room, looking at the clock as she did so. She knew that Julia would be itching to get on with tea before long.

'Ah, got it,' said Henry. He laid down the contents of his tile rack to reveal FAJITA. 'That J came up at just the right moment.'

Mollie returned to the table and looked as confused as Julia. Henry was prepared for it. 'A variety of tortilla,' he declared, a touch too pleased with himself. 'You fill it with spiced meat, cheese or salad.'

Mollie produced a mock smile. 'It's no use arguing, Julia. He's bound to have it right.'

Julia rolled her eyes. 'Oh I believe him. No need to check. I'll just see what I can do and then start getting some tea. After that I'm in the mood for some of Henry's bread pudding.'

Henry chuckled. 'And there is candied peel in it this week, Julia.'

'Very glad to hear it.' Already Julia's voice was starting to trail as she concentrated on her turn on the board. Henry recorded his score and replenished his rack with two further letters to compensate for those just laid down.

'Going back to what we were saying about getting up early for work,' said Mollie.' I was thinking about it the other day, and you talking about all your interests just now reminds me. When you came back from Saudi Arabia, you went to work at the old Dental Estimates Board.'

'That's right.'

'But recently at the Townswomen's Guild – another society I'm trying to get Julia to join, to reduce some more of her liberty......' She looked at Julia who smiled a little but her concentration was absorbed on the Scrabble board. 'I met a couple of people who had worked there and they said they stood it for a few months but that it was the most boring work they'd ever done.'

'Oh, it was,' said Henry. 'Four of us around a table checking every entry that came in from every dentist in the land; name, address, date of birth, date of examination. It all had to be checked before the dentist could get his money from the Government.'

'So why did you do it?'

'Following the caper in Saudi, and all the pressures I was beginning to feel in teaching after twenty years, that was exactly what I wanted. No responsibilities, no work to take home at night. For a long time it was golden.'

Mollie did not look convinced.

'I liked the setting so much. That was terrific compensation. A ten-minute walk from here or I could take the car if it was raining. On a pleasant day a huge field in the front to look at, the South Downs on the other side. I took sandwiches out in the lunch hour and could relax with no cares in the world.'

'I still can't imagine how a chap like you could have coped with such lack of stimulation.'

'Ah, but I had plenty of that in everything else I did. Besides which, I could finish work at 10.40 on a Friday.

Odd time but it meant a long weekend awaited. That was especially useful when I started doing the hospital radio programme. In those days I needed to spend a great deal of time preparing for it, so I used to get down there as soon as work finished, sort out the programme, come back home and start out again later. Then you both moved here, our Scrabble sessions started and by then I didn't need all that time to prepare a programme. No, that place, boring though the work was, suited me down to the ground.'

Mollie studied Henry. 'You really are a collected personality. I admire you for that. But 10.40 does sound odd as a finishing time.'

'As I recall, it arose from a convoluted arrangement of added hours during the rest of the week, so that there was a choice. I suppose they thought with the general boredom of the job, they'd have a stab at flexitime to inspire the workers. I jumped at the chance.'

Henry started shuffling around his collection of tiles, watching what Julia was about to do. She was showing signs of breathing hard as though she had found herself a word. He and Mollie both realised something was about to emerge.

'I wasn't there all that long anyway,' Henry continued. 'About five years. Then I decided I could manage on savings until my teacher's pension kicked in at 60. And there was the bonus of the people too. Quite funny, some of them, set in their ways, that sort of thing. But there were so many that I got to know a lot of them. I'd only just been chucked out of Saudi of course. I didn't make too much of it but some of those souls had seen the local newspaper reports. When they realised it was me, they were wide-eyed.' He chuckled. 'For a while I was looked on as some sort of celebrity. Daft really.'

'Got it.' Julia was triumphant. 'I can get rid of this valuable Z.' And so saying, she carefully laid out ZANY to coincide with the last A in Henry's FAJITA. Henry marked up her useful score. Julia sat back to draw breath from her exertions and the board passed on to Mollie. In her ebullient mood, Julia turned to one of the week's events.

'What do you think of Mrs May's performance in the Commons two days ago, Henry?'

'Impressive. And it made a change from Brexit.'

'Didn't it just? I'm fed up to the back teeth with that topic.'

'I think we all are now, Julia, regardless of our views on the matter. But it was astounding, wasn't it, what she said about the Salisbury poisoning?'

'I felt the gasp go up when she named the two individuals who turned out to be members of Russia's military and security services. How dare they cause all that havoc with their wretched, what was it, novichick?'

'Novichock,' Henry corrected.

'All that cloak and dagger stuff six months ago. Thousands of hours of CCTV study showing up what it did.'

Henry laughed. 'And then that madcap interview on Russian TV when they got back and why they had gone to Salisbury; describing it as though from a travel guide.'

'I think Mrs May was quite admirable in the way she reported it all, and then answered questions on it.'

'Yes, she did well there,' said Henry. 'I just wish she would deal with Brexit in the same way. All these deals she comes back with from Europe which everyone on all sides rejects.' He sighed. 'I suppose we will get an answer to it one day.'

Chapter 8a

❁

Al-Jum'ah 26 Dhul Hijjah 1439

'Astonishing, just astonishing.' Mollie spoke for all three of them as they stood together in the sisters' sitting room. It was al-Jum'ah afternoon, but all thoughts of Scrabble were far from their minds. Henry had brought the board and bag of tiles down as usual from his flat, together with all other items, but with one addition. It was a piece of paper, copies of which were being held in the hands of his two friends. They were standing in the middle of the room contemplating the contents.

'It's so impossible to believe he's coming right through here. Eastbourne!' Julia looked at the other two as she said it. They too looked up from their papers. It was not so much a letter as a usual command to be present.

'There's no question of a choice in it,' observed Mollie. 'We've all got to be there, haven't we?'

'I'm afraid so,' said Henry. 'But of course we're used to that.' He let the paper drop to his side for a moment. 'I didn't tell you in case it was gossip or a hoax, but I did hear about this possibility.'

The sisters looked at him questioningly.

'It was the chap I was telling you about, Muktar Ali, the doctor's brother. The first time I met him up on the downland. He said The Leader would be making a tour through southern England this month.'

'But it is so unusual,' said Julia. 'Coming all the way from Geneva.'

'Well, here it is in black and white. Next Tuesday. You realise the day's significance, don't you?'

Both sisters shook their heads.

'It commemorates the day all this started.'

'You mean it's 9/11 on Tuesday?' queried Mollie. Henry nodded. 'But how many years exactly?'

'Seventeen.'

'So it's not even a round number anniversary, unless it is in their calendar. I wonder what's really behind it.'

Mollie's intrigue had caught her sister's attention.

Julia laughed ironically. 'Perhaps it's a morale booster. Maybe The Leader is losing his grip.'

Her two companions turned to look at her in silence. 'No, it can't be surely.'

'Difficult to know what to think with these people,' said Henry. 'But nothing has been left out of this.' He looked down at the instruction sheet. 'All single women from this immediate area are to muster on the sea side of the corniche by the Wish Tower. And *we've* got to be on the other side, in front of the old hotels that used to be there, near Wilmington Square.'

'And then there are all these detailed timings,' observed Mollie. 'Single men must leave their houses and flats in this road at 14.15. We've got to follow on a quarter of an hour later.'

'Naturally,' said Henry. 'Couldn't possibly have us seen walking together in the streets.'

Mollie took careful note. 'But then we come to the dress code. Oh, how tiresome.'

135

'Yes, I see I shall be all right. All Muslim men are to wear their thobes. The infidels must put on their best with collar and tie and the lot. You ladies have to wear, guess what?'

'Oh, well, we're used to that in public,' said Julia. 'No surprises there.'

'Yes, but have you seen what our head gear has to be?' said her sister.

'No, I don't think so,' answered Julia vaguely. Then she spotted it. 'Oh, no. The niqab is bad enough, but at least it's possible to see through the slit. They're ordering us to wear the burqa with that damned mesh screen in front of the eyes. Oh, that's too much, in all those crowds too. What can they be afraid of with our eyes showing?'

'It isn't fear, Julia,' said Henry. 'It's another determination to show who's boss.'

Mollie looked at Julia and thought she was about to break down. She took hold of her sister's arm. 'Don't worry, dear. We'll get some practice in beforehand by going for some walks before Tuesday. And anyway you can hold on to me. I'll look after you and see you're all right.'

Julia was indeed about to whimper but pulled herself together. 'Quite right, Mollie. We'll get through it as with everything. It's all a lot of nonsense anyway. All these veils and scarves; they have absolutely nothing to do with the Koran. I gather there are no instructions in it to wear them at all. It's purely on the say-so of the men, as ever. Worried about their sexual desires being inflamed if women are seen without all the tiresome dressing up outside the home.'

'Well, of course you and I would be bound to have that effect on the men, Julia,' laughed Mollie.

Julia tossed her head aside. 'Now let's get down to some Scrabble.'

'That's the spirit, Julia.'

They moved to the table by the window and took up their usual positions. On this occasion all three seemed half-hearted in a way they had not been for a long time. Mollie opened up the board. In silence Henry passed the bag containing the tiles first to Julia. She plunged her hand in and took out a tile. Henry offered the bag to Mollie who did the same. Then Henry withdrew a tile. They each showed the result. Julia's tile was closest to A so all three placed their tiles back. Julia gave the bag a shake before retrieving several tiles. She counted out five and took two more. Then she passed the bag to Mollie. Disconsolately Julia shuffled the tiles around on her rack. The others did the same. Not a word was said between them. The only sound was that of the tiles being moved about on the racks. The ticking of the clock on the mantelpiece also seemed to take on an extra decibel. The three of them appeared to be concentrating on the task in hand but they all knew it was a matter of show. The clock ticking and the tiles rattling continued to be the only sounds. Compared with those, the sudden shriek of *Alluha Aqbar* from the loudspeaker at the end of the road came in like a roar through the window. The spell, such as it had been, was broken. Julia cried out.

'It's no use. I'm not in the mood for any of this.'

'Nor me,' from Mollie.

'It's obvious we all feel the same,' echoed Henry. 'Let's not bother this week.'

It was Mollie who took the initiative. 'Come on. We'll have a long tea break. Henry's bread pudding is ready and waiting for us. I'll make the tea this week.'

'We all will,' said Henry. They arose from the table as one, left the Scrabble set as it was, and Henry picked up the bread pudding to take it out to the kitchen followed by his two friends. They all jostled around in the confined space, Henry heading towards the cutlery drawer, Julia reaching for the kettle to take it to the tap, and Mollie arranging the cups, saucers and plates on the small table. They all got in each other's way and laughed.

Gradually over the next hour a sense of calm and resignation took them over again and they found peace and security in each other's company. The tea was made, the bread pudding was cut, and they repaired to the comfortable chairs and sofa in the sitting room, glad of their mutual friendship.

'You were saying it's seventeen years next week since it all started,' observed Julia. 'It was a Tuesday. I can't recall much more than that.'

'The weekend before sticks out in my mind,' offered Mollie.

'Mine too,' echoed Henry. 'What were you up to?'

'Something close to your heart. Broadcasting.'

'Really?'

'Do you remember Southern Counties Radio?'

'Certainly,' responded Henry. 'What were you doing with them?'

'Talking about the Campaign for Courtesy. They couldn't get anybody else. People were still on holiday. I had a sudden call on the Saturday night for a programme next morning. By that time I'd done a few things with you on hospital radio and felt fairly confident. But oh, that young couple running the programme. Cheryl and Jason, I think. From the small do-it-yourself studio the station had in those days in Terminus Road, I was supposed to be their sofa guest. It was hard to feel like that, cooped up in that space with headphones clamped on my ears.'

Henry laughed. 'Yes, there's plenty of make-believe with these things.'

'It was their banal chat, so inconsequential that I couldn't get on with. And their lack of knowledge. I happened to mention my film extra days and they latched on to that, wanting to talk about films. Do you know they'd never even heard of Ernest Borgnine.'

Henry laughed again. 'That's how it is as generations move on. But it's for the same sort of reason that I remember that last weekend of freedom.'

Julia and Mollie paid close attention as they poured out more tea.

'The Sunday the week before, we'd celebrated fifty years of Good Health Radio. And twenty-five since the station had been given that title. Big affair. The Mayor was there. So were various dignitaries from the national organisation for hospital radio. On the programme the following Friday I reviewed a lot of it. Had no idea of course it would be the last time I would ever do a programme again.

Julia and Mollie nodded sadly for Henry. They both recalled how much his broadcasting had meant to him. But Henry livened up with another memory.

'Do you know, I can recall the last record I played. It was the first record I ever bought, in 1960. The theme from *A Summer Place*. I had occasion to do so because one of its stars, Troy Donahue, had just died that week.'

Mollie let out a swoon of joy. 'My goodness, Troy Donahue! I had a poster of him in my room in the late Fifties.'

Julia rolled her eyes and all three laughed. So much did they thaw out that they decided they were ready once more for a further Scrabble session after all. In good heart they got up to take their places again at the table. As they did so, Henry spoke.

'You realise what else Tuesday is?' The sisters shook their heads.

'Not that they ever make anything of it. But it's the Islamic New Year's Eve. The following day we enter the year 1440.'

Chapter 9

✿

Tuesday 11 September 2018

Joyce Grimshaw was already standing at the corner of St John's Church in the district of Meads, Eastbourne when Henry clambered up the hill to meet her. Immediately she saw him she did not like the colour of his face as he fought for breath.

'Sorry if I've kept you waiting, Joyce,' he gasped.

'Don't worry about that,' she replied. 'But Henry, you don't look well.'

'I'll be..... all right in a minute.' He stood breathing hard. 'I'm late because I'm having a water softener installed, and they.....arrived later....than arranged.'

'Now don't try to talk. Is there anywhere we can sit down for a while?' Joyce looked around.

'Yes, we can go into the church gardens.' Henry almost forced the words out of his mouth. As he led the way, he held on to Joyce's arm. Her concern grew. Henry collapsed gratefully on to the park bench midway along the side of the church.

Henry smiled as his pallor improved. 'Oh dear, I used to manage that hill easily.' This was one of those occasions when he regretted not losing more weight.

Joyce attempted to make light of what was obviously troubling him. 'Well, it was probably because you were hurrying to meet me. How are you feeling now?'

'Better, thanks.'

'Sure you're able to go on with this? We could postpone it for another time.'

'No, no. I shall be fine in a moment or two.'

'Well, let's sit here for a while until you're on top again.'

'Okay.'

'Did you say you're having a water softener installed?'

'Yes.' Henry answered enthusiastically and his mind was taken off the slight pain in his chest.

'You won't regret it. That's one of the few things I still miss about Shropshire. The water is much softer there. When I came to London, I couldn't believe how hard it was. So I had a softener put in. You'll save a heck of a lot on cleaning liquid and washing powders.'

Henry looked down at his hands. 'I'll be glad to stop having such cracked skin. It's all right now in the mild weather, but my fingers are awful in the winter.'

'Yes, you should see a difference there too.'

Henry was clearly now breathing normally. 'Shall we make a start?'

'If you're up to it.'

'Yes, I'm fine.' Henry proceeded into his guide voice. 'Well, here we are at St John's Church. Most of it dates back to only 1957 as it was heavily bombed in the War.'

'Yes, I had heard about that. Just the tower escaped, I believe.'

'That's right.'

'But I'm amazed that they managed to blend in the new building so well with the tower.'

Joyce looked up and down the length of the church as they sat on the bench.

'Did well, didn't they? Let's get up and move on.' They proceeded out of the grounds back to the corner where they had met. 'Oh and by the way, do look at this spot. You'll see it clearly in the film tonight. You are still coming with us?'

'Rather. I wouldn't miss it. I remember as a child being captivated by Dr John Bodkin Adams. I still recall the day I came out of school in Ludlow and went into the paper shop with friends as usual to get the family's *Evening Standard*. We were all amazed at the headline: "Bodkin Adams Not Guilty". It seemed to put Eastbourne firmly on the map.'

Henry laughed. 'It did that all right. And strangely enough, it was the same year as this church was reopened.'

'Was it that long ago?' queried Joyce. '1957?'

'Afraid so.'

'What do you think? Was he guilty or not?'

Henry pursed his lips. 'I've given up trying to reach a conclusion. There seem so many arguments for and against. But I do know there are still relatives living of his patients who died who won't hear a word said against him.'

'Curious business altogether. Still, what else are you going to show me?'

'I thought we would take a stroll into the village and end up at the newest park here.'

'Sounds fine,' enthused Joyce as they moved off along St John's Road, she still a bit wary of Henry's condition, although he did now seem to be in a better state again. 'It's very good of you to take this trouble for me. Now I know you do this as part of your income. So let me know what I owe you.'

'Don't be daft, Joyce. It's a pleasure.'

The couple made their way along St John's Road, and Henry pointed out the house with a plaque on its wall. They went across to look.

'Cyril Connolly, eh?' said Joyce. 'He knew where to end his days.'

'Certainly did,' responded Henry. They moved on again and minutes later they were looking at another plaque, in Milnthorpe Road. Henry pointed out the house where Ernest Shackleton had once lived. From there he guided Joyce into All Saints' Park, which delighted her.

'This is lovely', she said. 'And you say it's only been here about ten years.'

'That's right. When they redeveloped this whole estate from the old hospital grounds into new apartments, there was a stipulation that a new small park had to be established.'

'I love these circular pathways,' Joyce observed. 'Makes the whole effect so much more interesting, along with the slightly hilly grass areas.'

'It's one of my favourites around here,' echoed Henry. 'Shall we take a walk through to the other end which comes out at the seafront?'

'Love to,' enthused Joyce.

The couple wound their way around and up towards King Edward's Parade giving out to the top of the cliffs. By then Henry was ready to sit down again and they did so on one of the benches on the greensward overlooking the sea.

Joyce took a few deep breaths. 'This is excellent. And the sun is trying to get through. So peaceful.'

They remained still and quiet for a few moments. 'I'm glad I met you and Mollie that day at the remembrance arch.'

'Yes, it gives you a bit of a focus every time you come down here,' replied Henry. 'And we're certainly glad to have your company.'

'I'm sure Mollie said that day that her sister was quite a bit younger than her.'

'Oh yes,' said Henry, 'by about ten years I believe.'

'Interesting,' observed Joyce. 'In some ways Julia seems the older of the two. Mollie is clearly fitter than she is, and does have a wider mind, I think.'

'I know what you mean. My feeling is that it has been more pronounced since Julia made the decision to give up driving three or four years ago. I suppose if people's attitudes are younger, they actually seem physically younger.'

'That must be what it is.' Joyce took a quick look at the front page of her newspaper. Henry spotted it and half-smiled to himself, remembering it to be the subject of a former encounter. He could not stand *The Guardian* but showed interest. 'Anything special today?'

'No, not really,' answered Joyce. They make reference to the anniversary of 9/11.'

'Of course,' said Henry. 'It's the eleventh of September today, isn't it?'

Joyce nodded. 'Seventeen years ago. Henry noticed the exasperation in her deep sigh. 'It's what set George W Bush off with his War on *Turr*.'

Henry admired her impression. 'Hardly the start. By then we'd already had the atrocities in Kenya and Tanzania.'

'I suppose so,' conceded Joyce.

'I still say the cause was the unfinished business over Kuwait.'

Joyce looked at him. 'Ah yes, Mollie was telling me that you were caught up in that.'

Henry nodded. 'Up to the point where I was given the sack.'

'Yes, I was taken with that. The quote in the paper of you accusing Aeronautics UK of collusion with the Ministry of Defence over a massive contract with the Saudi government.'

Henry laughed. 'You know I really did not say that. But a part of me could not help being delighted to be so misquoted. And it was your paper that did it.' He pointed to Joyce's lap.

Joyce tapped him on the arm. 'So they did something useful.'

Henry laughed again. 'Doesn't alter the fact that once Desert Storm had been won, if General Schwarzkopf had pressed ahead and gone into Baghdad to see off Saddam Hussein, the war in Iraq would not have happened.'

Joyce's back stiffened. 'That's a big "if", Henry.'

'Not really. The mandate from the United Nations stopped after Kuwait's sovereignty was re-established.'

'Quite right too. There'd been enough killing.'

'You think so? Because Schwarzkopf's hands were tied, there were thirteen further years of Saddam's atrocities before Bush and Blair went in.'

Joyce tossed her head before turning away from Henry. 'Don't talk to me about Bush and Blair. Warmongers.'

Henry remained quiet for a moment. 'I don't know about warmongers although I agree with you as to the outcome after Saddam had been deposed. The whole thing fell apart. But there was no question in my mind about their initial action taken in Iraq. And it was popular at the time.'

Joyce's eyes opened wide as she turned to him. 'What ever are you talking about, Henry? I went on the marches with my husband in London. On one occasion there were two million of us.'

Henry chose his words carefully. 'That's as may be, Joyce, but initially you did not speak for the majority.' He noticed that Joyce was starting to go red in the face so he spoke as softly as he could. 'I kept the statistics, have done all these years. The fact is that on the eve of war in March 2003, over 50% of the population believed the action was right. It climbed steadily and reached a peak the day Saddam's statue was pulled down in Baghdad. At that point 66% said the action was right. Even five months later at the height of the Hutton Enquiry debacle, when the majority thought we had been duped by the Blair Government, still 54% thought the right course of action had been taken.'

Joyce's mouth was now twitching. 'Yes, well, I wonder what the Iraqis themselves thought.'

Henry's voice grew even softer. 'I kept those figures too, Joyce. You would probably be surprised. In May 2004, a year after the war had ended, Oxford Research did a survey in the country itself. More than two and a half thousand Iraqis were directly asked if life was better then than before. A full 70% said yes.'

Joyce had clearly not expected that but the redness from her face began to diminish. For his part Henry was keen for the social pot not to boil over. In a conciliatory move he emphasised the area where they did agree. 'You are so right though about the aftermath. So much was squandered following the initial routing of Saddam. Between all of them, they ruined it.'

Joyce's mood softened. 'Well, for the rest, we must beg to differ.' She looked at Henry and smiled.

'Come on. Let's continue looking at Meads, and we'll finish up with a coffee at the Black Cat.'

'The what?'

'A delightful café in the centre of the village.'

They got up from the bench seat and continued their walk along King Edward's Parade, the sea on their left. Henry suddenly chortled. Joyce turned to him questioningly.

'I was just reflecting,' he said. 'This anniversary of 9/11.'

'What about it?' she asked.

'Well, I was remembering something about it that came to light in *The Times* a year or so ago.'

Joyce chuckled. 'I thought you were a *Telegraph* man. Like the sisters.'

'Oh we all are. But it was something in *The Week* that had been extracted from *The Times*.'

'What was it?'

'It's not funny, or wouldn't have been if an emergency had happened for us that day. In the event it sounded hilarious.'

'What did?' Joyce laughed through her impatience.

'It showed how unprepared we were if we'd been attacked that day instead of New York.'

'Really? How exactly?'

'It came to light through Richard Wilson.'

'Richard Wilson? Old Victor Meldrew in *One Foot in the Grave*?'

'No, no, Joyce. There was another Richard Wilson. The one who was Tony Blair's cabinet secretary at the time.'

'Hmm. I seem to remember the name vaguely,' murmured Joyce. 'What about him?'

'Well, it was his responsibility to ensure the Government was prepared for such attacks in Britain. But he discovered first that the Civil Contingencies Unit was away on a staff outing in Yorkshire. Then he found the entire Overseas Defence Secretariat was on a bonding exercise in Hertfordshire.'

'Heavens,' exclaimed Joyce. 'And you mean to say they were the two crucial bodies who'd have had major roles to play in the event of an attack?'

'Exactly, Joyce, according to Wilson. But that's not all. It seems a new upgraded government switchboard had only just been installed. And it crashed.'

Joyce started laughing as the pair turned off the seafront towards the village high street. 'You're right. It's not really funny, but it is. What a fiasco. I don't remember hearing any of this.'

'I asked Mollie if I could cut it out from the magazine. I've still got it. And it doesn't even end there.'

'Oh, surely not more foul-up,' protested Joyce.

'Apparently. Among other things Richard Wilson did was to check on the secret escape tunnel out of 10 Downing Street.'

'I never knew there was one,' said a surprised Joyce.

'It seems so. And when Wilson asked about it, can you imagine it? He was told that it was locked. Naturally he asked about the key.' Henry started laughing. 'He was told the keyholder had gone on holiday without telling anyone where he kept it.'

'Oh, doesn't that sound just like us?' said Joyce. 'Caught with our trousers down just at a crucial time.'

'Precisely,' answered Henry. 'Still. If you remember, Tony Blair hot-footed it straight back from the TUC Conference at Brighton that day just as he was about to make his speech there.'

'Back to save us all, eh?' Joyce and Henry continued chuckling as they made their way towards the Black Cat. 'I hope his way in through the front door of Number Ten wasn't impeded.'

Chapter 9a

Al-Thulathaa 30 Dhul Hijja 1439

Henry Wagstaff wrestled with his tie. He could not remember the last time he had worn it; there was nothing much to dress up for now. He looked in the mirror as he straightened himself with the unusual combination of collar, tie and jacket. He had bought the latter in recent years but now he could not button it up so he left it undone. Doesn't look too bad anyway, he decided.

He checked his watch. It was just coming up to 2.15. Time to go. The instructions had been clear enough. Men and women could not leave their dwellings together unless they were married or were brothers and sisters. That too was par for the course. Henry could not be seen to be in company with Mollie and Julia. He looked around and checked, and then realised that there was one more thing to do.

He took from his pocket the linen handkerchief he had placed in it that morning. He knew that on a day like this, the chance of a snap body search was high. He went to the bathroom and took from the handkerchief the cyanide pill he always kept with him. Everywhere he went, it went with him, even indoors, the equivalent of a lifeline around his collar with a disc to be pressed in an emergency. But not today. He could not risk letting his insurance policy be blown away. He thought for a moment before deciding to put the pill back in the handkerchief and return it to his bedroom where he placed it in a drawer, from which he took out another clean handkerchief. He closed the drawer and was ready.

He left his flat and started down the stairs. He heard movement inside the sisters' flat and knew they would not be leaving for another quarter of an hour. He nearly tapped on their door but thought better of it. He continued down the stairs and out of the front door. Walking along Chessington Gardens towards the corniche, he could see increasing numbers of other men doing the same. The crowds would be enormous. Except for many of the younger ones, nobody would want to be there.

Several flowing white thobes were apparent, but mostly the men looked the same as Henry did. As well as their dress appearance, they all conveyed a sense of resignation. Let's get this done with, seemed to be the order of the day. They would of course all spring to life when the motorcade came through, Henry included. The cheering would be intense, as though they were in North Korea. Henry had experienced one or two gatherings such as this before. It was all too nauseating to contemplate. But what else, in the face of armed soldiers and police officers, not to mention the cluster of CCTV cameras dotted around in places one could not even detect?

Following instructions, Henry made his way along Compton Street to the junction with Wilmington

Square. Before he got there, the queue started. Slowly he edged forward until able to turn right leading towards the corniche. One by one they went through the barrier where their identity cards were carefully checked. Hard-nosed officials looked from the photographs on the documents to the faces they represented. Each one was shown to another official standing close by. This individual looked at some sort of pad in front of him that Henry did not recognise and could only assume was part of new technology to which the rank and file were not privy. At all events the official seemed to insert in his pad the number that appeared on the identity card. He it was who then gave the respective recipient the nod to move on. Henry was one of a dozen men who were instructed to turn right at the corniche and move to what had been the Lansdowne Hotel. They were commanded to mount a set of steps to the right of the old main entrance and stand there. Henry was not impressed with the positioning. His party would be in full view. There would be no question of letting up on the cheering of The Leader as he came by.

Mollie and Julia Chadwick were making their own way into Compton Street in the opposite direction to Henry's. Silverdale Road was inevitably closed off as it ran alongside the Ramada Hotel so that the ladies had to join all others on the climb up South Cliff Avenue to reach the sea front and follow instructions down to the promenade and cross over to the sea side. The sisters were thankful this was not taking place at the height of summer. In their restricted clothing, the exercise would have been difficult. At the top of South Cliff Avenue, they had to join a queue and go through the same procedure as Henry. They showed their iqamas to officials, all of them men, so that there was no question of checking facial identity. But their numbers were checked off and the sisters were equally intrigued as Henry had been by the use of a hand-held pad where their pass numbers were apparently entered. Then they were told to follow the line across the road just past the Ramada Hotel to stand in front of the Western Lawns. They were ushered into their places by stern officials, ready to push anybody into submission the moment any sign of resistance showed itself. Julia nudged Mollie.

'There's Mrs Johnson a couple of rows in front of us.'

Mollie sighed. 'How can you be sure? She'll be covered from head to toe like us, and there are a lot of people in between us.'

'Oh, I would know that angular stance anywhere. Did I tell you about meeting her outside the pharmacist when you were in there on al-Sabt?'

Mollie remembered it well but she knew she was going to hear it again so she shook her head vaguely.

'She was just going inside. I made the mistake of asking her how she was. She leaned forward in that conspiratorial way of hers and said quietly: "The doctor's very worried about me". Very worried! What time has Dr Shefik got to be worried especial.....'

But Mollie had already switched off. She was giving all her attention again to the atmosphere, disturbing because it was so enthusiastic. She stared across to the Ramada Hotel, which was looking more ornate and downright vulgar with all its gold trimmings than when it was The Grand. Even now The Leader would be waiting to make his entrance from it on to the public arena.

Henry surveyed the scene. He had a good view of one hundred and eighty degrees. The children were being escorted, school by school into their places on the kerbs of King Edward's Parade. The crowds were becoming thicker. As always, nothing was being made of the New Year, just as the old western new year celebrations had gone by the board. Henry's mind travelled back to the scenes in Trafalgar Square years before, the gongs of Big Ben, Jools Holland on the television, and before him Andy Stewart. All of it a thing of the past. Most people would not even know when the thirty-first of December occurred now, including the Chadwick sisters, who would be in their places somewhere opposite him about now. As for Big Ben, that was demolished in the original attack, a day after the Twin Towers in New York.

He sighed as he looked around again. There was the depressing aspect of it building up. The young people were getting excited. Not just the children but the younger adults. The looks on their laughing faces depressed him more than Henry could begin to describe.

Like Henry, Mollie and Julia on their side of the road could only feel increasingly depressed by the reaction they were witnessing in their midst. The children from their various schools were laughing and enjoying the occasion. So were the young adults. They wondered if the converted Tony Henderson was close by with little Fatima and his unspeaking wife. They really did all seem to want this life, with its structure, its discipline, its codes, where nobody had to decide anything because all decisions were made for them.

Mollie was suddenly put in mind of an old film, *The Stepford Wives*. That was it, where everyone was conditioned into doing everything. Her mind wandered. How she would have loved to be involved in that. She had enjoyed working with Bryan Forbes on *Séance on a Wet Afternoon*. But he had made *The Stepford Wives* in America and there was no hope of.....Oh, what was she going on about? All in the past. There was too much of the present to contend with.

Nobody spoke to each other in Henry's section. Men on their own had long realised the necessity to keep their own counsel. As he looked around him, Henry used the time for reflection. He was thankful it would be only a short ceremony. The motorcade would be hurrying on to Bexhill and Hastings and then they would all be instructed to disperse. His bladder would be sure of holding out during such a time scale.

Then he pondered again about The Leader. Apart from the pomposity of the title, he was glad it had to be deployed at all times. He could not bear to use the appalling man's name. But he considered again where he was making the journey from. For some reason Geneva had been selected as the centre of European control. Henry smiled ironically to himself when he considered that the city bore the name of the great Convention on war ethics. It certainly bore no relation to the ethics of The Occupation. There was irony too in the easier task the oppressors had experienced in mopping up the countries of Europe. With the EU in place, they could reach the various systems far more easily. Henry had always wanted to leave the European Union. Now with the new masters it was unceremoniously dismantled anyway.

Which led him on yet again to trying to work out how the Islamists had got together. The amount of burying of the hatchet between Iraq and Iran alone must have been monumental. But he had seen something of it in the lead-up to Desert Storm in 1991, when after eight years of war between the two, Iranians said they would come to Iraq's aid against Saudi and the allies. Crazy. Then there was the settling of theological differences between the Sunnis and the Shias. He shook his head as he thought anew of the impossibility, as it would have seemed at one time, of their all coming together under the influence of the Wahhibis. All of it for the sake of central control, and of getting rid of the royal House of Saud. Henry sighed again.

Suddenly a roar went up from the direction of the Ramada Hotel. Several cars emerged from the wide seafront entrance on to the corniche. The crowds were into their stride. The motorcade progress was at a snail's pace, so that the full force of the occasion could be appreciated. Then the simultaneous cry began collectively. 'Leader! Leader! Leader!'

Even at this point, well before the main arrival, the frenzy was whipping up. The half dozen men by Henry's side on the steps were being taken over by it. He remembered how aware he should be of the soldiers and officers in plain clothes mingling in the crowd. One or two might even be immediately next to him, monitoring his performance. The CCTV cameras would be in full swing. He looked up and around and of course could not see any.

Henry too started shouting, as much as his cracked voice would allow him. The first of the five or six cars had reached him. Nobody had a clue who the dignitaries were travelling in them. Not that it made any difference to the cheering crowds. The young people were shouting themselves hoarse. Henry waved along with them and became concerned. Was he pretending or was he becoming wound up by herd instinct? The idea frightened him.

There was a brief pause. Then what appeared to be the last limousine made its way even more slowly towards him. The crowds were beside themselves in ecstasy. He looked closely into the back of the car.

Across the road, the same car had reached the full view of the sisters. They peered inside it. There in the middle of the back seat, almost lost in it, was a hunched senile figure, entirely still. He did not wave. Mollie was shocked to see him looking far older than his eighty-one years. She thought of another of the films she had worked on, reminded forcefully of *El Cid* already dead but strapped to his horse and ridden out to battle to reassure his troops. A similar sight confronted her now. The car passed slowly, the crowds continually shrieking. She turned to her sister who at the same time had turned her face to Mollie's. No words were needed. They were thinking the same thing.

'*Was* it him? The Leader? Was that really Saddam Hussein?'

Chapter 10

✿
〽

Friday 29 March 2019

'Leave the washing-up, Mollie,' Julia called out. 'The vote is coming up.'

Mollie took off her rubber gloves and left the kitchen to come back into the sitting room where Julia was glued to the television set.

'I reckon we could do worse than to follow Henry's example in getting a water softener. He must have had it about six months now and he swears by it. Perhaps we wouldn't have to invest so much in washing up gloves.' But her sister did not hear. She was absorbed.

'I must say, Julia, for someone who voted Remain, you're increasingly interested in what's going on with this Bill.'

'I just want to see them getting on with it. It's been nearly three years now and we're no further forward. Let's get it settled and leave the EU and be done with it.'

'I agree, dear,' said Mollie. 'But I can't see it happening this afternoon, even with the third vote.'

'I expect you're right. And to think we were supposed to leave tonight. Someone counted up twenty-eight times or something that Mrs May said: "We leave on the twenty-ninth of March." Yet still no sign of it.'

On the television screen the Speaker of the House of Commons was on his feet, producing his rapid-fire delivery. 'As many as are of that opinion say Aye.' The roars went up for both sides, upon which John Bercow shouted: 'Division!' The wave of more than 600 Members of Parliament began streaming out of the Chamber towards the division lobbies.

'I can't think what has possessed Henry to go up there today.' Julia picked up the *Daily Telegraph* lying beside her on the sofa. Henry had left them with it on his way out to London in the morning.

'Well he had set his heart on it months ago,' said Mollie. 'When they didn't cancel the celebration rally, he was still determined.'

'Yes, but Mollie, all those crowds of people, at his age, being overweight and so on.'

Mollie smiled. 'The vote won't come in for another quarter of an hour. I'll just finish washing up.' She got up from the chair by the door and replaced the rubber gloves she was nursing over her hands.

Julia was absorbed again in the article that had caught her eye before lunch. 'You know, Mollie, I just don't understand the world today.'

Mollie smiled again, this time to herself. It was a phrase Julia used increasingly these days. But she had to admit, equally increasingly, she found herself in agreement with her sister.

'What have you spotted this time, Julia?'

'It's this new transgender or transsexual rights group, or whatever they call themselves. They're talking now about doing away with the words he and she, putting in something like ze instead. Can't think how they would even pronounce it. I mean it's nonsense. We won't even be able to talk about men and women soon. I tell you, I can see a time when parents won't be able to refer to their children as sons and daughters. What will they say instead?'

Mollie's inspiration was caught. 'Possibly something like the progeny, or perhaps even the begatted. Not to worry though. The so-called woke generation can try all they like to tell us what to think. But they can't stop us thinking what we *want* to think. I'll just finish up in the kitchen. Give me a shout when the vote is declared.'

'How long shall we be able to act on it though?' queried Julia. 'I've just read about a faction somewhere advocating that all of us over about seventy should no longer have the right to vote in elections.' She laughed. 'They might as well go the whole hog and say we should all be gently done away with on reaching that age.'

Mollie stopped and turned in the doorway. 'Don't entirely rule it out, Julia. It happened in *Soylent Green*.'

'In what?'

'About the mid-70s, dear. Charlton Heston and Edward G Robinson.'

o o o

In spite of his dislike of London now, Henry Wagstaff was glad to be in the capital today. He had been a touch apprehensive about going to Parliament Square for the rally, weighing up how safe he would be in the crowds. On the other hand he had wondered whether it would be crowded at all. One never knew with these occasions. In the event when his eyes had fallen on the scene, he had no further cause to doubt on that score. But he did have cause to doubt how long his bladder would hold out. The nearest lavatories were in Westminster tube station and were ghastly, probably through overuse. He was glad to find he was managing so far.

What had really propelled Henry to be there and forsake his Friday afternoon Scrabble session with Mollie and Julia was that it should have been the day the country would take its leave of the European Union, at eleven o'clock this very night. He felt filled with frustration. It was galling that it was not happening.

A mass of humanity was thronging the vast green area in front of the entrance to the Palace of Westminster. The Remain side's rally the previous Saturday afternoon had been enormous. While not nearly as large, this sea of faces covering Parliament Square and its borders was impressive. As was the mood. People were smiling at each other. There appeared to be good humour along with determination.

Right outside the entrance to Parliament, Henry asked a young police officer if they would be 'kettled' as used to happen. He was alarmed by the possibility. The officer was certain they would all be free to come and go. But he suggested that as it was likely to become even busier, Henry would be advised to stay on the outskirts if he wanted to get away quickly. Henry followed the policeman's advice, eschewing the chance to get further into the action. He was depressed to note the atmosphere marred by two past-their-prime skinheads sporting the hand-written entreaty on their backs: 'Fuck U, E.U.' In disgust he turned away from the sight of their bullish necks throbbing away with barely concealed rage beneath their prematurely bald heads. Henry was reminded again of Rattigan's line in *Separate Tables*: 'The trouble with aligning yourself to a cause is that you so often have to associate with such disagreeable people.'

His state of mind was immediately remedied by the sight of Steve Baker standing at the kerb, a couple of enthusiastic supporters either side of him. Henry moved across to him to thank him for all he was doing. A roar was ensuing from the area by the wide platform that had been erected on the side of Parliament Square nearest to St Margaret's Church. Mark Francois was the first to speak, reporting that less than one hour earlier, the E.U. Withdrawal Bill had failed for the third time to pass through the House of Commons, with the help of the likes of himself because it was so weak in terms of Britain's rights.

Henry continued to be impressed by the speeches, from Claire Fox, Kate Hoey and Peter Bone. He was less impressed, not because of the speech but by the apparent messianic adulation shown towards the final speaker, constantly interrupted by the herd-like chants of 'Nigel! Nigel! Nigel!'

The speeches over, Henry decided to take a rest by moving towards a low brick wall near some trees on the edge of the Square. He was glad to sit down as his chest was feeling tight and his breathing was a problem. He had some difficulty talking to a quiet and charming lady, also sitting there and on her own from Marlow as he discovered. But he managed to keep up a conversation with her.

After a few minutes they were alerted to a cheer going up. They looked round to find it coming from Victoria Street and moving into Parliament Square. A small group was marching in. The lady beside Henry was elated. 'Oh look, 'she said. 'It's a group from France waving their Frexit banners. They must be our equivalents. I didn't know we had any.'

Henry's attention was diverted from his chest pain. 'Yes, I had read about them. It's invigorating, isn't it? And look at the way they're being received.'

People were cheering them and going up to them.

'Oh, I am pleased,' said the lady. 'What a welcome for them. That should give the lie to the charge that all of us are insular and xenophobic.'

There was a contented smile on her face as she got up to tell Henry how much she had enjoyed meeting him and would she excuse him?

It was much to Henry's relief that she stood up to take her leave so that he could gather himself again. His chest pain gradually subsided and his breathing returned to normal. Instead of making his way back to Victoria Station straightaway as planned, he decided to soak up more of the atmosphere, for there was still plenty of it.

He made for College Green, a familiar sight from the television screen, and was uplifted to find the squad from France arriving at the same time. They were cheered by the enthusiastic crowds who advanced on them so that they had to stop marching. They comprised all age groups and the goodwill shown towards them was striking. Henry was one of several who shook hands with them. He chanced his shaky 'O' level French on them, offering: '*Bienvenu a Londres*.' One chap put his hand on Henry's shoulder and mouthed back a whole lot that was beyond him until he finished with the name 'Charles de Gaulle'. Henry attempted to look convinced and pleased with the man, not that he had ever been a fan of the General.

The lady from Marlow had been right. Sharing the same views of the European Union, the two factions could not have been more pleased to see each other, and they were showing it.

Henry spotted a familiar face. He could not think of her name but she was the French commentator who sometimes broadcast on *Newsnight*. She always amazed him with her perfect English pronunciation, in contrast to his own indifferent French. Henry waited until she had finished interviewing one of the be-suited Frenchmen, and he was then unable to resist congratulating her on her work here. She seemed enchanted.

It was as Henry was moving away from the immediate scene that he felt a pain in his chest far more searing than the first half an hour earlier. He sank to the ground. Two women were close by and knelt down beside him. He had enough power in him to feel incensed by the usual ridiculous question that had become commonplace at such times, especially in all the banal soaps: 'Are you all right?' What did it look like? Henry heard someone else raising the alarm on his phone. Despite the woman's silly question, he was grateful to her for loosening his collar as he was aware of beads of perspiration dripping down his face. He also started shaking uncontrollably.

It seemed like an age, even for those attending to him. The other woman produced a plastic cup and a bottle of Lucozade. Henry saw it and immediately liked the idea. But before his thirst could be quenched, two St John ambulance people appeared from nowhere to take over and they advised the helping women not to give Henry anything until the paramedics arrived.

Henry felt a sense of determination brewing inside him. 'I'm not going yet,' he said to himself. 'I'm damn well going to live to see Brexit done.' He could vaguely hear the muffled sound of an ambulance siren in the distance before lapsing into welcome unconsciousness.

o o o

'Well, that's that,' observed Julia, getting up from the sofa. 'Powerful speeches in Parliament Square, I have to admit. But I wonder where we go from here.'

'We seem to have been saying that for a long time,' sighed Mollie. 'We can only wait for developments, and the next deadline. Can't see Mrs May lasting much longer though.'

'I'll make some tea.' Julia moved towards the kitchen and looked at the clock. 'Henry said he would aim for the 5.15 train. More crowds in the thick of the rush hour. Won't do him any good. Should be home about seven. Then perhaps next week we can get back to our Scrabble.'

Chapter 10a

☼

Al-Jum'ah 22 Rajab 1440

'Well, it's six months now since the Grand Tour, the big occasion with the motorcade.'

Mollie and Julia both looked up on hearing Henry's comment.

'Is it really?' queried Mollie. 'In their calendar's terms it must be seven. I lose track.'

'Quite,' replied Henry. 'And in that time, have you noticed things have died down a bit?'

'Not so that *I've* noticed,' offered a distracted Julia.

'Well, we haven't had the raft of instructions coming to us at anything like the usual rate.'

'I suppose not,' said Mollie, equally distracted by the contents on her tile rack.

'I just have this feeling that things might be on the cusp of a turning point.' The sisters sat up.

'I don't want to build up hopes and if anything is in the wind, it will take a long time.'

'What makes you think so?' asked Julia.

'A couple of things in the paper this week. There's the prediction that shale gas is starting to reduce.'

'Yes, I did read that,' said Mollie. 'But they reckon they've got supplies for the next five years at least.'

'Sure, but that's not very long in the scheme of things. And there was another item, printed very small and I'm surprised they put it in at all.'

'What was that?'

'The meeting between The Leader and his counterpart covering Asia and Australasia. They used the old western fallback: "A fair and frank exchange of views". We've never had a trace of that before. Frankly, I've been waiting years for something like that to happen. It never seemed likely that Saddam and Osama bin Laden could last for ever on good terms. And anyway, we all saw what The Leader looked like last year. He can't last too long. Say what you like, I think it could be starting to unravel. Things like that can often be a sign.'

'What, you think we might be through with the Occupation?'

'Oh, not for a long time,' said a more subdued Henry. 'It won't happen in our lifetime. And if it does, it won't be rosy. When occupiers know that their time is heading towards the finish, scorched earth policy sets in, not least with people. Think of the added atrocities in Nazi Germany, and with the Japanese towards the end of the War. Not to speak of the transitional period. You only have to think what happened when African countries became independent. It took years in some cases. And look at the Soviet Union dismantling in 1991. Unemployment set in. So did the opportunists. It won't be a cake walk, whatever form it takes.'

'In that case,' said Julia morbidly, 'we're probably better off going on as we are until our time comes.'

Despite himself Henry could not help agreeing with his friends. All three sighed in resignation. They had long given up hoping and it had worn them out years ago. Not that it altered their general everyday mood, good and bad.

Of the latter and over a period of eighteen years the Scrabble threesome had found the five stages of grief a decided reality. Denial had certainly begun the process in those early days of Occupation: the sense of disbelief in the face of the impossible that had become anything but. The next stage, anger, was the one in Henry's case that had never gone away. So much of it was there in fact that, setting aside the third stage for the moment, he had never reached the fourth: depression. He had seen a lot of it around him and he caught it in the sisters' eyes at times, although they rarely voiced it. The fifth and final stage was one that Henry was convinced he would never reach: acceptance. Julia had tried it once or twice, with her expression of relief, for example, that people could walk around the town at night without hindrance. And for most people the financial side of things was golden. Pension increase, good wages all resulting from shale gas, up to now, as well as energy from the harnessing of the coastal waters. They all had a good life economically. Nobody was homeless. In any case for the youngsters growing up, this life was the norm. Anyone under twenty would have had no knowledge of what had gone before, including the internet, long decreed as far too menacing. Many young people didn't even know what one was talking about when trying to explain about e-mails.

Yet it was the third stage of grief that was the most interesting, described as an attempt to bargain one's way out. Out of what? In Henry Wagstaff's view it had more to do with compensation. In their three cases it took the form, one way or another, of a change in physical condition. Julia's way was to crash out sometimes with the most acute migraines. She had never suffered in such a manner before the Occupation. She thanked heaven that they never lasted more than a couple of days.

And now on this Friday afternoon, the twenty-ninth of March 2019, the date Henry had specifically checked before coming down to the sisters' flat, the weaknesses in both Mollie and himself, the compensations, were to come to the fore. As they sat together at the table, Henry felt acutely sorry for Mollie. Her face was still blotchy from the rashes she had already been suffering, but added to them were others, awful sores on her hands and arms. As ever with these sudden outbursts she treated them with resilience, but she kept scratching them and made them bleed.

'Don't, Mollie' said Julia, quietly and kindly. 'You'll make them worse, dear.'

Mollie pulled herself up and said she hadn't realised she was doing it. She would see the doctor again next week. That was another thing. Medical services were now second to none, and they had all agreed that Dr Shefik al Katatni was one of the best they had known, always thoughtful and wanting to know about the whole person. There was no question of limited time during consultations. He had never managed to diagnose Mollie's occasional rashes but as they always subsided with the variety of creams and ointments he prescribed, she said she would prefer not to go to hospital to find out more. As she looked over her rack, Mollie winced. Henry asked her if she was all right. He realised it was an idiotic question. Of course she wasn't. Usually one to make light of these things, Mollie laughed as this time she said no. It was clearly hurting her.

'Do you want to go and lie down, Mollie?'

'Oh no, Julia. This helps to take my mind off it.'

Henry could feel again the anger rising in him. This was his own compensation, a luxury in which he had hardly if ever indulged before the Occupation. It did not happen too often, but it had proved a problem occasionally when in company with the sisters. They had grown to sense it, and did so now. Henry was becoming quieter. The cheery smile was no longer on his face. The sisters exchanged an uneasy look that signified an agreement to humour Henry if necessary. Time for some playacting. It was Julia's turn. She laid down her letters.

'What ever's that, Julia?' exclaimed Mollie.

'What does it look like?' Julia had seen BOXES displayed on the board and had decided to add to it. She affected to show more exasperation than she usually did at being challenged.

'LETTERBOXES,' she declared proudly.

'That's not one word,' said her sister.

'I'm sure it is. I've seen it only recently. What do you think, Henry?'

Henry was no longer in the mood to try and keep the peace in their sisterly tussles, and he assumed this was another one of the same. 'I can certainly vouch for the halfway stage,' he said wearily. 'The word had a hyphen in between in Dickens' time. It crops up in *Great Expectations*.'

'That surprises me,' said Mollie. 'But anyway, hyphenated words don't count in Scrabble.'

'Let's settle this in the usual way,' sighed Henry, reaching for his dog-eared OED. Arriving at the root word, he went through the various forms of it. 'It isn't one word according to this. Other than "lettering" and "letterhead", all other forms are in two words.'

'Oh, well, I suppose that settles it,' conceded a disgruntled Julia, taking the six relevant letters back off the board. 'I know I've seen it somewhere recently though as one word.'

Henry appeared to be thawing out again but it was not to last. 'That's a surprise,' he mused partly to himself.' He still had his nose in the dictionary.

'What's that?' asked Mollie as Julia's face was buried again in her next possibility, thankfully aware that Mollie had apparently stopped being conscious of her rashes.

'Well they haven't completed the definition of letter boxes.'

'How so?' said Mollie.

'They just say it's a box or slot into which letters are delivered.'

'That's right. What else is it?'

Henry laughed scornfully. 'We all know it's more than that. It's the box you post letters in to send off.'

'Never,' exclaimed Mollie. 'They're called post or pillar boxes.'

'Well I've always called them letter boxes as well.'

Mollie might have left it alone. She didn't. 'Oh that's daft, Henry. Post boxes are red. Letter boxes on house doors aren't.'

'Ours is,' said a now truculent Henry.

'That's pure coincidence,' countered Mollie. 'We decided to have the front door painted red years ago and the decorator just happened to include the letter box.'

In other circumstances all parties would have let go of the situation. Henry's particular weakness in these oppressive times failed him. His own attempt to bargain in the face of grief, his own compensation of anger, kicked in. The result was irrationality.

'Well I bloody well call them letter boxes.' His shout filled the room and his fist came down so hard on the table that he scattered some of the tiles.

Immediately there was total quiet. The sisters looked at each other with their mouths open. No one was more shocked than the perpetrator of the scene. Henry was too embarrassed to think of anything to say, let alone that he was sorry.

In the stunned silence Henry heard a familiar sound, even though it was muffled. He choked out the words. 'That's my entry phone sounding. I'd better go up and see what it's about. Might be important.'

He got up awkwardly, consumed with embarrassment, and slunk out of the room across the hall and out of the apartment door. He leaned against the wall on the landing for a moment, confused and ashamed of his outburst. Then he looked up the stairs to his flat. Rather than climbing them to check his entry phone, he decided to go straight down to answer the door.

Inside the sisters' flat, Mollie and Julia exchanged a sad shrug. With a half-smile Julia said she would go and make the tea. Left to herself, Mollie looked out of the large bay window but could see no sign of anybody, not that it was possible to spot who might be under the porch canopy at the front door. She stayed peering out of the window, emitting a sigh as she gazed up and down Chessington Gardens. She noticed a police van across the road several doors away. Nothing strange in that. They drove around all the time, usually with the religious police, the mutawa, determined to keep pious order. She turned back to the table and made some attempt to assemble the letters that Henry had scattered in his loss of temper but inevitably could not recall accurately all the placings.

Henry, descending the stairs, was pulling himself together. He was still acutely embarrassed and ashamed but he resolved to apologise profusely when he returned to the sisters and echo the refrain he was sadly becoming accustomed to: 'I don't know what came over me.' By then he had reached the front door and now opened it.

A western-dressed Arab man with a moustache as severe as his face stood on the doorstep. '*Salaam aleikum,*' he said.

'*Aleikum salaam,*' mumbled Henry, parroting the required response.

'Mr Henry Wagstaff?' he asked officiously.

'That's me.' Henry was beyond showing even forced deference to his masters. But he was thrown by what came next.

'You are the same Henry Wagstaff who worked in Dhahran in 1989 and 1990 for Aeronautics UK?'

'That's right.' Henry was on full alert.

'You were there at the time of the invasion of Kuwait?'

'That too is correct.'

'You wrote an article for the local paper here in which you insulted His Late Majesty King Fahd ibn Abdul Aziz al Saud.'

Henry weighed his words before answering. 'It was not long after fourteen hundred pilgrims had been trampled to death at the Hadj pilgrimage at Mecca. I observed that the then King had declared the tragedy to be an act of God.'

'Indeed you did. You had no right to say such a thing. Then you compounded the felony by saying you had no faith in the King because of it.'

'As I certainly didn't. But why are you dragging all this up now? As you have just said, I wrote it in the local paper here, well before the Occupation, not in an Arabic paper.'

The official's lips tightened. 'That is not the point, Mr Wagstaff. You wrote it.'

'In any case,' observed Henry, recognising that he had nothing to lose now, 'you were dead set against King Fahd yourselves. You deposed the entire royal house and placed them in the same cells from which you released the seven hundred Shi'ites languishing there for years. Why on earth are you standing up for King Fahd now, after all this time?'

The official was clearly annoyed. 'He may have been a nuisance, Mr Wagstaff, but he was *our* nuisance. We are compelled to follow up all cases of insurrection, no matter how minor they might be, no matter from how long ago.'

'I see. A case of *pour encourager les autres*.'

'What?'

'Nothing.'

'Your attitude does not serve you well, Mr Wagstaff. There will obviously be repercussions.'

Henry had no idea what would come next. It could be something light or harsh. At the age of seventy-nine he was no longer bothered about dying, or rather the point of death. This life had nothing left to offer so he might as well accept the alternative. But he was curious. It had not been the Saudis who had expelled him from the kingdom all those years ago, but the company for whom he had been working. It was they who had got wind of the newspaper article and spirited him away on a flight back to England before the Saudis found out. With its £10 billion contract to supply Tornados and personnel, Aeronautics UK was bound to cover itself.

As Henry was reflecting on this, he noticed the official turn and signal towards someone further along the road. Henry was out of sight of the four uniformed men emerging from a van.

'Just for the record,' said Henry. 'How did you find out?'

'By chance. Someone you once worked with decided to be loyal to her masters.'

'You mean I was betrayed?'

'If you insist on putting it that way.'

Henry wracked his brain. He had only ever talked about it to the sisters, certainly since the Occupation.

His oppressor continued. 'We arrested a woman recently. She was having an affair with a man not her husband. She worked with you at the former Dental Estimates Board.'

Henry began to see the picture unfolding. Transgressors were sometimes given the option to name names for a lesser punishment, like the old McCarthyite days in the Fifties.

'Don't tell me,' said Henry. 'You wanted to know of anybody who might have form.'

The man did not know what Henry meant. 'We asked her if she knew of anyone who had or might have opposed us. She told us your story and that it had appeared in the local paper. She didn't know which year it was but that it was at the time of the Iraqi invasion of

Kuwait. Our team went through the papers of 1990 and soon came across this.'

The man produced a copy of the page Henry had penned in August 1990. He could not resist a chuckle at the irony. Of all things to let him down, it had to be himself, with the help of the newspaper editor who had accepted the story. It was a repeat of the cause of his dismissal from the kingdom.

'What will happen to the woman?'

'She will not now pay the ultimate price.'

That news gave Henry cause for a degree of relief. Not quite Sidney Carton from *A Tale of Two Cities*, but he felt a sense of peace that the woman would not be stoned to death. Nor could he feel any sense of blame towards her, whoever she was. He would prefer not to know who had let him down. She would serve a long prison sentence and be in purgatory for the rest of her life at having betrayed Henry. For himself, whether it was the law of inevitability setting in, a sense of philosophy or whatever it was, he was feeling a certain calm he had not known for years. As he reflected on his readiness to face the course of action he was about to take, he saw four police officers arriving on the scene. The oppressor provided an explanation.

'Two of these gentlemen will now go up to your flat and search it thoroughly. You will come with the rest of us.'

Time to act. As he stepped out of the doorway, Henry affected a severe sneeze. He reached into his pocket and made a point of displaying the linen handkerchief he kept there. He covered his nose with it and in the middle of the piece of cloth he made contact with the cyanide pill. His teeth bit firmly into it. The last stage of grief: acceptance.

One floor up Julia had arrived back in the room with the tea trolley to find Mollie's face buried in the Oxford English Dictionary. 'I see you have managed to get some of the tiles back in order,' she laughed awkwardly.

'It's quite right what Henry discovered Julia. "Letter boxes" are two words.'

'Do you know, Mollie, I realise now where I'd seen it?' Julia lowered her voice. 'I won't say anything about it when Henry comes back up. It was in the *English Arab News* only this week. We might still have it. They were announcing another one of their tiresome edicts and it said that a document would be coming through our letter boxes soon.' Julia laughed. 'If they'd only let us carry on having our PCs and e-mail, they would have saved themselves all their trouble, and paper. But the point is they printed it as one word: letterboxes. I *knew* I'd seen it recently.'

'Just goes to show, dear. You can't believe everything you read.'

The sisters heard a lot of movement on the stairs and raised voices. 'Henry must be bringing somebody up. Oh well, that's the Scrabble over for this week. Perhaps it's just as well. It'll give him time to cool down a bit.'

'In any case, he'll be fine by tomorrow,' observed Julia. 'He'll be up here in the morning full of remorse and standing at the door with a massive bunch of flowers. You'll see.'

Notes

Some names of people and organisations are fictional. The following are not.

p.1   David Dimbleby, 1938 – present. British journalist and commentator.

       Keith Vaz, 1956 – present. Former Labour Minister.

p.2   Paddy Ashdown, 1941 – 2018. Leader, Liberal Democrats, 1988 – 1999.

       David Cameron, 1966 – present. British Prime Minister, 2010 – 2016.

       Jeremy Corbyn, 1949 – present. Leader, Labour Party, 2015 – 2020.

       Nicola Sturgeon, 1970 – present. First Minister of Scotland.

p.3   Ann Widdecombe, 1947 – present. Former Conservative Minister.

p.6   Nato: North Atlantic Treaty Organisation.

p.7   Emma Thompson, 1959 – present. British actress.

p.8   Elisabeth Kubler-Ross, 1926 – 2004. Swiss-American psychiatrist credited with identifying the five stages of Grief.

p.9   Winston Churchill, 1874 – 1965. British Prime Minister, 1940 – 1945; 1951 – 1955.

p.12   Salman Rushdie, 1947 – present. Indian British novelist.

p.14   Wahhabis: Islamic sect practising Wahhabism.

p.21   Ed Balls, 1967 – present. Labour Shadow Chancellor of the Exchequer, 2011 – 2015.

P.27   Ronald Reagan, 1911 – 2004. United States President, 1981 – 1989. Formerly film actor.

        Jerry Lewis, 1926 – 2017. American comedian and actor.

p.36   Chris Jordan, 1968 – present. Artistic Director, Eastbourne Theatres, 2000 – present.

p.41   Roy Jenkins, 1920 – 2003. Labour Home Secretary, 1965 – 1967; 1974 – 1976. Comment attributed in *The Independent*, 4 March 1989.

p.42   Hugh Gaitskell, 1906 – 1963. Leader, Labour Party, 1955 – 1963.

p.43   Anthony Eden, 1897 – 1977. British Prime Minister, 1955 – 1957.

        Gamal Abdul Nasser, 1918 – 1970. Egyptian President, 1956 – 1970.

        Desmond Morris, 1928 – present. Zoologist and author.

p.47   Theresa May, 1956 – present. British Prime Minister, 2016 – 2019.

Muammar Gaddafi, 1942 – 2011. Libyan Leader, 1969 – 2011. Comment attributed in *The Week*, 4 September 2010.

p.50   Balcombe: West Sussex village. Site of once proposed shale gas development.

p.54   Richard Attenborough, 1923 – 2014. British film actor and director.

p.57   George Osborne, 1971 – present. British Chancellor of the Exchequer, 2010 – 2016.

p.78   Malcolm Muggeridge, 1903 – 1990. Journalist and broadcaster.

p.84   Thobe: long ankle-length Arabic male garment.

Ghutrah: Arabic male headdress.

p.94   *Quatermass II*: Science-fiction serial by Nigel Kneale, televised 1955; subsequently a film.

p.96   Saddam Hussein, 1937 – 2006. Iraqi President, 1979 – 2003.

p.97   Pythonesque: reference to *Monty Python's Flying Circus*, 1970s British television comedy series.

p.98   Fahd ibn Abdul Aziz al Saud, 1921 – 2005. Saudi Arabian King, 1982 – 2005.

Eric Heffer, 1922 – 1991. Labour Housing Minister, 1983 – 1984.

Arthur Mullard, 1910 – 1995. British comedy actor.

Eli Wallach, 1915 – 2014. American stage and film actor.

p.99   Zsa Zsa Gabor, 1917 – 2016. Hungarian American celebrity and actress.

Henry Fonda, 1905 – 1982. American film actor.

Sidney James, 1913 – 1976. British comedy actor.

George Cole, 1925 – 2015. British stage, film and television actor.

Gloria Swanson, 1899 – 1983. American film actress.

Dame Edna Everage (Barry Humphries), 1934 – present. Australian comedian.

Yasser Arafat, 1929 – 2004. Palestinian Liberation Organisation Chairman, 1969 – 2004.

Alfie Bass, 1916 – 1987. British film and stage actor.

Bella Emberg, 1937 – 2018. British comedy actress.

p.104   Douglas Hurd, 1930 – present. British Foreign Secretary, 1989 – 1995.

p.108   Tom King, 1933 – present. British Defence Secretary, 1989 – 1992.

Neil Kinnock, 1942 – present. Leader, Labour Party, 1983 – 1992.

Gerald Kaufman, 1930 – 2017. Labour Shadow Foreign Secretary, 1987 – 1992.

p.109   Margaret Thatcher, 1925 – 2013. British Prime Minister, 1979 – 1990.

p.121   Heather Rennison, quoted in *The Independent*, 28 February 1991, by journalist Robert Fisk, 1946 – 2020.

p.128   John Bodkin Adams, 1899 – 1983. Eastbourne physician acquitted of murder, 1957.

p.130   Dental Estimates Board: Government body based in Eastbourne from 1948, dealing with all national dentistry formalities until closure in 2006 when computer operation took over.

p.139   Ernest Borgnine, 1917 – 2012. American film actor.

p.144   Cyril Connolly, 1903 – 1974. Writer and literary critic.

Ernest Shackleton, 1874 – 1922. Explorer.

p.146   Desert Storm, 16 January – 28 February 1991. Allied operation resulting from the failure of Iraqi forces to withdraw from Kuwait despite United Nations orders during the build-up identified as Desert Shield, 2 August 1990 – 16 January 1991.

Norman Schwarzkopf, 1934 – 2012. General, United States Central Command, 1988 – 1991.

p.148   Richard Wilson, 1942 – present. British Cabinet Secretary, 1998 – 2002. Comment attributed in *The Week*, 10 December 2016.

p.161 Charlton Heston, 1923 – 2008. American film and stage actor.

Edward G Robinson, 1893 – 1973. American film actor.

p.162 Terence Rattigan, 1911 – 1977. English dramatist.

p.163 Steve Baker, 1971 – present. Conservative MP.

Mark Francois, 1965 – present. Conservative MP.

Claire Fox, 1960 – present. Director, Institute of Ideas.

Kate Hoey, 1946 – present. Labour MP, 1989 – 2019.

Peter Bone, 1952 – present. Conservative MP.

Nigel: reference to Nigel Farage, 1964 – present. Leader, United Kingdom Independence Party, variously from 2006 – 2016.

p.168 Osama bin Laden, 1957 – 2011. First General Emir, al-Qaeda.

p.176 McCarthyite: description given to policy and action of Senator Joseph McCarthy (1908 – 1957) and the House Un-American Activities Committee in 1950s Washington.

9 781839 756931